THEIR SUN WAS GOING NOVA

They were already colonists of a planet far from Mother Earth. They had been there several generations, they had built their cities and their homes and had tried to construct their better Earth . . . and then came the alarm.

Their new sun, the star around which their brave new world revolved, was about to explode. All who could must flee—with only hours to spare. Any spaceship available, any crew, anyone who could go out into the uncharted cosmos must do so at once.

Their ship got off . . . Its crew was makeshift, the refugees' talents were poorly mixed, and there was but one among them who knew what was required to tame an unknown planet.

But they did not know he knew. And he did not know whether he dared tell them.

POLYMATH

by

JOHN BRUNNER

DAW BOOKS, INC.

DONALD A. WOLLHEIM, PUBLISHER

1301 Avenue of the Americas
New York, N. Y.   10019

Published by
THE NEW AMERICAN LIBRARY
OF CANADA LIMITED

First Printing, January 1974

1 2 3 4 5 6 7 8 9

PRINTED IN CANADA
COVER PRINTED IN U.S.A.

◆ | ◆

"One thing about those damn winter gales," Delvia said in a make-the-most-of-it tone. "They did give us a bit of stored power to play with."

"But they took so much more away from us," muttered Naline.

"I guess so. Still, not to despair. We may find things aren't as bad as we expected." Delvia cut the accumulator out of circuit and the whine and thump of the air-compressor died. With capable fingers she uncoupled the latest cylinder from the pipe, checked that its pressure-gauge was operative by bleeding a few pounds off—the air screeched thinly as it escaped the valve—then dropped it with a clank against the two already lying on the strange greenish sand. Taking an empty one, she began to connect it up.

"You can take those three, Lex," she added.

"Right," Lex acknowledged. "Finished, Naline?"

The darker girl, "baby" of the surviving refugees, nodded and turned to catch the eye of the lined-faced man standing a few paces distant along the beach. "Ready for you now, Captain!" she called, pushing back her long black hair behind her shoulders.

Captain Arbogast seemed to return from a long way away. He had been staring out across the blue calm sea of the bay to where a polished arc of metal showed above the water. He moved mechanically now and came to join Naline.

Lex, his lean tallness emphasized by the odd-looking garb he had on, gathered the three full air-cylinders into his arms. He was wearing a spacesuit, the fluorscent orange fabric of which—designed for maximum visibility in space—was almost blinding under the blue-white glare of the morning sun. Naline had tied bands of black, glistening elasticon around his limbs and trunk to gather

5

the slack of the material. It had been meant for someone much more heavily built.

He picked up his helmet, gave it a rapid wipe to dislodge some grains of blown sand which had adhered to the sealing-ring, and addressed Arbogast.

"I'll go down and see if the boat's ready, Captain."

"Go ahead," Arbogast answered. His voice sounded dead, and there was no expression on his face. He seemed unable to tear his gaze from that glistening thing in the sea.

"Left wrist, please," Nadine said. She was performing the same service for him as she had just done for Lex. Arbogast's suit was his own, but the past winter's privations had cost him a good twenty pounds of his former weight. Obedient as a puppet, he lifted his arm away from his side.

The compressor started again, and Delvia straightened to her full height. Glancing at Lex, she said, "I do envy you. After the winter I feel dirty clear through. Nothing I'd like more than a long cool swim."

Well, she was dressed for it—or rather undressed. She had on nothing except a ragged red tabard open down both sides. It was obvious that being half starved had merely fined down her former statuesque proportions; her flesh was firm and shapely, and good muscles moved under her sleek skin. It was reassuring to find that some at least of the refugees were capable of remaining healthy here. Although rubbing the noses of the less-fortunate in the fact might lead to problems later on. . . .

"I shouldn't try it," Lex replied soberly. "Not after what happened to young Bendle."

Delvia nodded and grimaced. Unconsciously she lifted one foot from the ground, supporting herself with a hand on the compressor, and used its sole to scratch at her other calf. Lex looked more closely. There was a reddened area.

"Del!" he said. "Are you itching a lot?"

Embarrassed, she dropped her foot to the ground. She said, "A bit. Sunburn, I guess."

"Then what are you doing in that skimpy rag? What do you want, a case of lupus from the high ultraviolet? This isn't—" He broke off, acutely aware that both Naline and Arbogast had turned their eyes on him. He had been going to say, "This isn't Zarathustra, you know," And that, of course, was a stupid comment.

He licked his lips. "You ought to be wearing a whole-body garment, Del," he finished.

For an instant he thought she was going to snap at him, tell him to mind his own business. Instead, she sighed.

"I know, I know. I'm blonde, so it's foolish not to. But after the winter it's unbearable! I'm not joking when I say I feel filthy inside. I never wore the same clothes for so long in my life. It's as though the dirt's worked its way down to my bones!" She gave a shudder. "But you're right. I'll ask Doc Jerode if he can give me a screening ointment."

"You'll be lucky," Lex murmured. With a nod to Arbogast, he turned away.

Behind him he heard Naline utter a grunt of exasperation. "Del! Do you have any scissors?"

"Not me, but I know who has. Why?"

"I'll get you to chop this hair off for me. Keeps falling in my eyes. The job's fiddling enough anyway—only one kind of knot will do, and if I don't get the tension right the bands either slip off or constrict the circulation. . . ." The words tailed off into a mutter, and Lex caught nothing more.

He felt almost cheerful as he approached the spot where Aldric and Cheffy were inspecting their makeshift boat for leaks, despite what he was afraid he and Arbogast were shortly going to discover on the bed of the bay. The gray chilly fogs and the appalling gales of winter had been like a prison for the spirit; now, almost literally overnight, they were released and a summer stretched ahead of them as long as an Earthly year. They had endured the worst their new home could throw at them, and most of them had survived. Even some of those who had thought they would never plan for the future again once their birthworld had been calcined were beginning to act like human beings instead of frightened animals.

Inland, in the cleft-valley where they had huddled for shelter along a riverbank, damaged houses were being mended and new ones planned. Here on the beach a dozen people under the leadership of gray-haired Bendle —recovered from the shock of losing his son last fall— were carrying out a methodical survey of the rocks and pools. Everything was changed, of course. The winter gales had done more than spin the windmills for weeks

on end. The dunes, the shoals, even the huge rocks
scattered like currants in a sand-pudding had been stirred
into a new arrangement.

Nonetheless, the situation felt—well, promising.

Here and there on the beach were brownish, greenish,
and reddish pieces of organic debris. Bendle's team had
looked at these first. Most were harmless fronds of a
rooted sea-plant, torn up by the last storms. Those which
were mobile and possibly dangerous, though dying out of
water, had been marked with a warning splash of white
paint, and one had been pegged to the ground with a
sharp stake. A circle had been scraped around it in the
sand.

Lex paused and examined this creature. Like many of
the sea-beasts, it wasn't easy to kill. Pinkish and greenish,
quadrilaterally symmetrical, leaking a sour-smelling fluid,
the staked body humped and pulsed; the paired flexible
trunklike organs which were limbs, gullets, channels of
excretion, and reactor-pipes combined writhed vainly
toward him, extending almost but not quite as far as the
circular groove.

A long cool swim . . . Lex shuddered and strode on
briskly.

"Admiring our prize exhibit?" Aldric called, turning
his dark glasses as Lex approached. He was a stocky
redhead, and had been fat. But no longer. Nobody among
the refugees was fat this spring.

"You could say so," Lex agreed, setting down his air-
cylinders with his helmet on top. "Anyone invented a
name for it yet?"

"I want to call it *polystoma abominabilis*," Cheffy said.
He didn't raise his round head, capped with close-curling
black hair. He was using a hot-spray to apply quickset
plastic to a pair of pegs projecting from the rim of the
boat's peapod hull. His other hand held a spatula with
which he was shaping the pliant material before exposure
to air hardened it rock-solid. "That," he added, "means
the disgusting thing with a lot of mouths."

"Apt," Lex murmured. "Any leaks, by the way?"

"Not now. Two or three cracks we had to seal."
Cheffy shut off the hot-spray, gave a final dab with the
spatula, and stood up.

"What are the pegs for?" Lex said. "Rowlocks?"

"Yes, of course." Aldric kicked at a pair of long, wide-
ended objects lying in the boat's shadow. "The free

paddles we were trying last year weren't very efficient, you'll recall. Nor the punting-pole."

Lex gave a dismal nod. It had been when his punting-pole stuck in bottom-mud that young Bendle had fallen overside and never come up.

"So I've been putting these together in my spare time," Aldric went on. "Theoretically, they should drive a loaded boat better. We've hung a tiller on the stern, too—there. Not that I'm going to make any guarantee, you realize. *I* never expected to have to cobble together primitive make-shifts like these. If it hadn't been for Cheffy's interest in Earthside history, I don't imagine I'd ever have dreamed of making oars."

Lex nodded. It wasn't the first time that Cheffy's purely intellectual awareness of subtechnical devices had had to be translated—generally by Aldric, who was a deft craftsman—into hardware improvised from anything to hand.

Momentarily depressed again by the colossal scale of the task they'd taken on, he said, "What makes you so sure we're going to have a *loaded* boat?"

Aldric looked out to sea. "She has settled, hasn't she?" He sighed.

"Sunk is more the word," said Cheffy. "Probably sifted half full of wet sand into the bargain. You'll be working in at least a dozen feet of water, Lex."

"Luck's been with us so far," Lex countered with forced casualness. "It may not be as bad as you think."

Cheffy snorted. After a pause, he said, "How do you imagine the others made out? I gather Ornelle's been trying to raise them by radio, without success."

True enough. Consequently no one was giving much for the chances of the only other refugees known to have reached the sanctuary of this planet. He was sorry Cheffy had mentioned the subject; he'd hoped that everyone would be too busy for at least another few days to worry about the party whose ship had landed—or crashed—on the inland plateau.

"Gales must have been terrible up there," Aldric said, reaching for the stern of the little boat. "Well, let's push her to the water. The captain ready yet, Lex?"

Shading his eyes, Lex stared back along the beach toward the air-compressor.

"Just about, I guess," he replied.

The last band was tied. Critically Naline passed her

hand over the slick surface of the suit, touching the knots in turn. As she felt the one on Arbogast's chest, she gave a murmur of surprise.

"Are you all right, Captain?" she demanded.

"Of course," Arbogast grunted. "Why?"

"You're shivering," Naline said. In the act of laying down the latest charged cylinder, Delvia glanced around.

"Nonsense," Arbogast said. He stepped back, avoiding the eyes of the girls. "Is my air ready, Delvia?"

"Yes, three cylinders."

Arbogast bent stiffly to pick them up, paused while Naline—still looking worried—placed his helmet on them, uttered a word of thanks, and headed for the waiting boat.

Looking after him, Naline said under her breath, "I hope he doesn't have a fever. You can't see it, but his whole body is—well, sort of vibrating."

"That's nothing to do with fever," Delvia said. She turned quickly to the compressor and disconnected the accumulator leads from its motor, then picked up and began to unfold the solar collector sheets. "Give me a hand to spread these flat, will you?" she added over her shoulder.

Moving to obey, as she always obeyed Delvia, Naline said in a puzzled voice, "But he *is* shivering, I tell you. And in full sunlight."

"Not shivering. Trembling." Delvia pegged down the corners of the first sheet and coupled the accumulator leads to its output terminals.

"What? Why?"

"The ship—what else? All winter long he's talked about nothing except patching her up and getting her aloft. Now he's come out and seen what's happened to it. He's grounded."

"Aren't we all?" Naline countered bitterly.

"He's a spaceman. I guess that makes it tougher. And he isn't so young anymore." Delvia brushed sand from herself.

"Besides," she went on, "don't you remember when things began to get bad at the start of the winter he kept trying to persuade everybody to take shelter in the ship?" She gestured in the direction of the thin shining arc which was all of the vessel now showing above water. "How'd you like to be in there? Come on—I'll trim that hair for you now."

◈ **‖** ◈

"Air," Aldric said, checking the items of gear over the stern of the boat. "One, two, three cylinders. Weighted belts. Boots—"

"Last time," Lex realized suddenly, "we were just walking on the bottom. But these are ordinary magnet-soled spaceboots. I don't want to be dragged feet first against the hull every time I go close."

"Thought of that," Cheffy said briefly. "I told Aldric to change the magnets for chunks of lead. But we couldn't find any. He had to make do with plain steel. Go on, Aldric."

"Net bags. Lex, don't pick up anything which we'll have to haul up on a cable, will you? I'm not sure how stable this boat is, and I'd hate to be tipped into the water. One waterproofed handlight. At least it says it's waterproof. Two hatchets, the best we could think of in the way of weapons. There is absolutely *no* means of making an energy gun fire under water. Cheffy tells me they used to use compressed air for underwater guns, so I'll get to work on one as soon as I can think of something expendable enough to use as ammunition."

"Don't expend it," Lex suggested. "Use something long enough to tie a cord to. We have plenty of that."

"There are things down there," Aldric countered sourly with a jerk of his thumb at the sea, "which I would not care to be tied to if they took off for deep water. Of course, if you want the thrill of a submarine joyride in the wake of a hurt and angry monster. . . ?"

"Point taken," Lex said, and grinned.

"I'm glad. We don't want to lose more people than we have to. And what do you think of our new anchor?" Aldric held up a shiny metal object consisting of a shaft and four spiked, curved tines. On the shaft was a coarse spiral thread, and fitted loosely on this was a rotating collar bearing four sharp blades.

11

"If this gets caught in bottom-weeds, or some beastie tries to cling to it, you haul on the cable sharply, that releases this spring catch—see?—and the blades spiral up the shaft." He gave it an approving pat and placed it in the boat.

"Cheffy, are you going with them, or shall I?"

"I'll go. You can make the next trip." Cheffy swung his legs over the side of the boat. "Push us out a few yards, will you? And mind where you put your feet."

Lex scrambled lightly aboard and took the bow thwart. "OK, Captain," he called to Arbogast.

But Arbogast was staring toward the sunken spaceship again, his hands hooked together in front of him, his knuckles bright white. He didn't seem to have heard.

"All set, Captain!" Aldric said sharply.

Arbogast let his hands fall to his sides. He swallowed hard before speaking. "I . . . I changed my mind. I'm not going."

"What?" Aldric took a pace toward him. Cheffy, startled, paused in the act of setting the oars in the rowlocks. Only Lex, slewed around on his thwart so he could see the captain, gave a slow nod. He hadn't been altogether unprepared for this.

Arbogast bowed his head and walked off up the beach, his dragging feet leaving smeared marks. The dying horror pegged to the ground sensed his passage and hunched once more to try to strike at him.

"Now just a moment!" Aldric said hotly, starting after him. "You can't leave Lex to—"

"Aldric!" Lex launched the name on the air like a dart. "Aldric, let him alone."

"The hell!" Aldric snapped. "Look—it was his idea he should go, wasn't it? Are we to waste another hour finding a suit to fit me or Cheffy, have it tied up, go hunting for different boots? It took most of yesterday to find enough wearable kit!"

"Keep your temper," Lex said. "Think of it his way. How would you like to go see your old home wrecked and smashed, with alien creatures crawling in every corner?"

"Did I suggest it? Did I?" Aldric wiped his face. "And —hell, talk about homes being wrecked and smashed!"

"Calm down, Aldric," Cheffy said. "Lex is right. At least we don't have to *see* what's become of our homes." He spat over the side of the boat.

Aldric drew a deep breath. "OK," he said resignedly. "Let's go hunt out a suit for me."

Lex hesitated, thinking wryly how just a few minutes ago he had rebuked Delvia for taking risks. But—he excused himself—a survey of the ship was essential before tomorrow's assembly, when they were due to take stock of their resources. He said, "I can go down by myself."

"You're crazy," Aldric said. "Without a phone? When we don't know half the species of sea-life around here? When it's likely the rutting season for things as dangerous as that multilimbed horror Bendle had to nail down? You're apt to wind up as stock-nourishment for a clutch of eggs!"

"I'll keep my hatchet in my hand. Oh, get in the boat!" Lex was suddenly impatient. "We need to know what's happened inside the ship!"

And, as another argument struck him: "I did two dives last fall, damn it, and the captain hasn't done one before. It's quite likely safer for me on my own."

Aldric shrugged. "OK—but I don't have to like it."

He bent to the stern, leaned his full weight against it, and pushed it free of the sand. It rocked violently as he jumped aboard. For a minute or so Cheffy fumbled with the oars, finding them hard to synchronize; then he abruptly got the hang of it and the boat began to move steadily over the calm water. On the beach Bendle's team paused in their work to watch.

Arbogast was plodding on without turning. Lex saw Delvia and Naline talking agitatedly, obviously about the captain; he hoped neither they or anyone else would run after him demanding explanations.

Determinedly, he looked ahead toward the tarnished but still-gleaming spaceship. It was possible to see how the curve continued below the surface, but it would be some time before they were close enough to tell what part of the vessel was uppermost. As a mode of progress rowing a boat was apparently inferior even to walking.

"It's moved five hundred yards at least," Aldric said from the stern. "Lex, how do you imagine it traveled so far?"

"Rolled, I guess. Too heavy to have floated out." Who could have predicted that on a moonless world—hence effectively a tideless one—no beach was stable? There were no meteorologists among their panicky handful of fugitives; in fact there were hardly any trained personnel, so that a dilettante like Cheffy and a hobbyist like Aldric had emerged as leaders where technical matters were concerned. He went on, "If I remember the old layout correctly, that whole stretch of ground where the ship rested must have been undermined. And we know the bottom shelves gently. As soon as it rolled enough for the locks to admit water, there was nothing to stop it sinking deep into the seabed. Must have been as fluid as a pumping-slurry with the currents."

"If only the locks hadn't been open," Cheffy said. "Remember the noise? Wind blowing across the opening, making the whole ship sing, as though it were playing the organ at its own funeral. I hope I never hear anything so eerie again."

Lex and Aldric were silent for a moment, remembering not only the noise—which they would carry in mind until they died—but other things. Arbogast losing his temper when he realized what the sound was, and attempting to reach the ship in a ninety-mile gale with waves breaking over the hull. And railing against the fool who'd left the locks open, until it was worked out he must have done it himself, because he had been trying to persuade everyone to shelter aboard during the winter instead of trusting themselves to ramshackle huts of planking and piled dirt.

"Why did we pick this place, anyway?" Aldric grumbled.

"Reckon we'd have done better on high ground?" Cheffy countered.

"No. No, probably not. Lex, what do you suppose has become of the others? Think they lived through the winter?"

"Maybe. Don't see why not, in fact."

"I don't see why," Aldric put in. "They haven't contacted us since the storms gave over, have they?"

"They could simply have lost their antennas," Lex said. "Remember, they did at least have the ship's hull for shelter. A gale could hardly have made that roll."

"So I hear," Cheffy said. "Like a squashed egg! And wasn't Arbogast pleased? Thinking he'd put down badly until he saw what the other captain had done. What's his name—the other captain, I mean?"

"Gomes," Lex supplied. "Yes, the ship was badly cracked."

"And," Aldric said, "they'll have had subzero temperatures much longer than us. They're probably iced solid, half buried in snow—at least the salt spray off the sea kept that from happening to us. But there were chunks of ice in the river until two or three days ago."

"You don't have to tell us," Cheffy said. Trying to look over his shoulder, he lost control of the oars and had to fight to stay on his thwart. "Hah! I wan't designed for traveling backward. How much farther?"

"We're past halfway," Lex said.

"I'll row back to shore," Aldric offered. "Who knows? The boat may be lighter on the return trip instead of heavier."

Something snapped at the port oar a second later, as though to underline the grimness of his humor. When the blade lifted again, it carried with it a writhing creature, wet-shiny pink in color, which had sunk its fangs in the wood of the blade.

"Damned nuisance," Cheffy said in a resigned voice. "Aldric, I told you these things ought to be made out of metal. Aluminum for choice. Hollow, too."

"When I get my electric furnaces rigged, I'll let you know," Aldric retorted. "Can you shake it off?"

Cheffy shipped the starboard oar awkwardly, then put both hands to the other and flailed it around. The creature emitted a gush of yellow fluid that discolored the sea, but clung fast.

"Turn the oar around," Lex said, picking up his hatchet. With some difficulty Cheffy complied, and Lex knocked the beast flying. It had left puncture marks in the wood, deep as nailholes.

"Having second thoughts about diving alone?" Aldric inquired.

Lex shook his head. "Those teeth wouldn't get through the suit fabric—though if there's any strength in the jaws I could get a nasty pinch and a lasting bruise. But from the way it struck at the oar, I suspect that species preys on fishingbirds. Which reminds me!" He sat up straight, eyes searching the sky. "Where are they? This bay was full of them last fall!"

"Perhaps they're migrants," Aldric offered. "We'll probably see them back now the weather's turned."

"Seen any landbirds?" Lex asked. "I saw a few yesterday."

"Me, I wouldn't have noticed. Been too busy since the thaw. We can ask Bendle about that when we get back." Aldric turned the tiller a little and peered past Cheffy.

"Getting close now," he reported. "Have the anchor ready, Lex."

"Right." He picked it up carefully, avoiding the scythe-like blades. That would certainly shock any bottom-prowler which tried to hang onto it. An unsuspected trap. Like the one which had sunk their starship.

He hadn't answered Aldric's question—"Why did we pick the place?"—any more than Cheffy had. They'd chosen it because both sea and land teemed with life, offering a double range of potential foodstuffs; any ocean is a repository of salts, and if they couldn't eat the native protoplasm or needed to supplement it, then simple processing of seawater would provide trace-elements for the diet-synthesizers; there was a rivermouth running back into a sheltered valley, and near fresh water was a logical site for a settlement; there were treelike growths, and wood was a material you could work with handtools. . . . Oh, the choice hadn't been made lightly, and in almost every way it was a good one.

Mark you, the way in which it hadn't been good might conceivably prove disastrous.

Now, in the clear water, he could see far down the curving side of the hull. At about the limit of vision there were soft darknesses and a motion not entirely due to the changing angle as the boat rocked. Lex shivered.

I'm not cast in the right mold for a hero.

Last summer, when they had improvised their underwater technique for the recovery of Bendle's son, it had been easy. He hadn't given a second thought to the obvious logic of the plan. Air, an impervious suit, boots that proved just right to keep the feet down, weights on a belt—and straight ahead with the job.

But he'd had a lot of time for second thoughts during the winter.

Still, this too was something that had to be done. "Stop rowing, Cheffy," he said, pleased with the levelness of his voice. He cast the anchor overside; it sank, gleaming, as he paid out the cable. Mindful of the spring-release activating the knife-blades, he gave it only the gentlest of tugs to seat it, then knotted the cable to the bow-pin.

"Here's your belt," Cheffy said. "Put it on while I hitch up your air."

"Right."

Belt. Boots, hatchet, handlight, net bag. He weighed about ten pounds short of neutral buoyancy; he would sink gently to the bottom. When he wanted to return, he would discard the belt and rise slowly, or open the valve on both air-tanks wide, filling the suit so full it would shoot to the surface like a bubble. Easy. Why was he sweating so much? Because of what he was now convinced he would find?

"Air's coupled," Cheffy said.

"Right—wish me luck." Lex set his helmet on his head and with a quick twist seated it against the sealing-ring. For better or worse, this was it.

◆ **III** ◆

Her eyes were red with lack of sleep, her voice was hoarse from addressing the dumb microphone, and her head was swimming so that the words she spoke no longer seemed to mean anything.

All of a sudden Ornelle reached the end of her endurance. She thrust the microphone away from her, put her arms on the cool smooth surface of the table, leaned her head on them, and began to sob. Like the tip of a cracked whip she had been jerked through a cycle of emotions for which she was simply not fitted.

She wished she was dead. Like the others.

Once there had been a planet called Zarathustra; people said comfortably, "Zara." There were two hundred and ninety million people who said it. Figures of ash rose in Ornelle's mind, marched across a blazing desert that had been fertile ground. A burning child screamed. She had not seen that. To stay so long would have meant she also burned.

Zarathustra had ended in such nightmare that—had it been a dream—those who dreamed it would have clawed themselves, threshed wildly about, tried to throw their bodies to the floor rather than slip back into sleep and see more horror. It had been incredible—the sun was yellow-white each day as always, round, usual. You didn't see the change. But in the observatories someone said a word: nova. Someone else said: how long? The machines gave the answer.

Soon.

Then into the calm pleasant settled life chaos and terror reached like a scythe into grass. Go now, they said. No, not stopping to take anything. No, not to look for children or parents, not to find a lover or a friend. *Now*.

And if you didn't, they had no time to drag you. *Go*.

White-faced officials. Spacemen moving like machines. Machines moving like men in panic, emptying the holds of cargo vessels on a spaceport in darkness. Useless goods being hurled aside, trucks and helicopters moving in with canned and dehydrated foods, medicines, bales of clothing. Diet-synthesizers being charged with trace-elements. All the time, everywhere, screaming, wailing, and sometimes a shout of savage anger begging a moment's peace and silence. People shoveled like broken toys into the bellies of the shining ships.

And then the light breaking under the horizon and the knowledge that on the dayside of Zarathustra heat like a torch was shriveling life away.

Then those who had not acted for themselves or been passive like Ornelle, bewildered into letting action be performed for them, *felt* the truth and came weeping and howling, naked from bed, clamoring like wolves for survival. But the ships were full; the ships were lifting into space.

In the crowded holds there had been time to think of those who were left at home. There was a terrible oppressive darkness, not physical but in the mind. Later she heard of other ships with which contact had been made, overfilled, where the oxygen was inadequate and the refugees stifled, where the lance of sickness ran through hunger-weakened bodies. But in the ship where she was, there was just enough.

Not much was learned of other ships, though. For some reason Ornelle didn't understand, to get clear of the continuum distortions caused by the nova shifting fantastic masses of matter over giant distances at appalling speed, it was necessary to run ahead, under maximum hyperphotonic drive, in whatever direction they chanced to select.

In fact: into unknown darkness.

At the season when its sun exploded, Zarathustra had

been on the side of its orbit farthest from Earth and most of the other human-inhabited worlds. It was a recently-opened planet—indeed, Ornelle's own parents had been born on Earth and had emigrated when they were young. The idea of trying to beat back around the nova and approach a settled system had been considered, but it was impossible; their ship was a freighter, not one of the passenger expresses disposing of as much power as a small star.

Then, pincered between the narrowing jaws of shrinking fuel reserves and the limits of the ship's internal ecology, the only hope was to find a planet—any planet —with supportable gravity and adequate oxygen. One system in sixty had a planet where human beings could survive; about one in two hundred had a planet where they could live.

At the end of their resources, they had touched down here to find summer ending. They had no time to determine whether this was a one-in-sixty or a one-in-two-hundred world. At first only the lashing scorn of the few who intended to survive at all costs had driven the majority to behave as though there were hope. They felt themselves not only isolated, but abandoned, even condemned.

The arrival of a second ship from Zarathustra, that landed on a high plateau inland, was like a new dawn. Abruptly life, not just temporary survival, seemed credible. While with sudden demonic energy the refugees worked to build a crude town of wood, sun-dried clay and scraps from the ship, a team made its way inland to the site of the other landing to ask news of friends or relations.

There were none; the other ship was from a different continent on Zarathustra. Still, its mere presence was comforting; a radio link was organized on an agreed frequency and for the rest of the summer and the brief autumn they kept in touch.

The vicious speed with which winter had slammed down had prevented a second expedition being dispatched to the plateau; moreover, weakened by carrying a huge burden of ice, their main antenna had collapsed in a gale months ago. But directly it had become possible to re-rig it, they had powered the radio again. Ornelle—to whom the presence of other human beings on this world signified something; she couldn't have described it—had waited feverishly to learn how they had fared.

When intermittent calls had been made for some days,

most people were resigned to giving the others up for lost. But Ornelle had insisted on being allowed to continue, and since she had no specially valuable skills they had let her go on. Now she had spent three long days and most of three nights calling, calling, calling—and hearing nothing. She might have thought that the radio was unserviceable, but she could hear her own voice from a monitoring receiver across the room.

This wasn't life she had secured, then—so it appeared to her. It was mere illusion. The strange planet must already have killed half the intruders from space. It was only a matter of time before it ground the rest of them down.

She had tried to convince herself that if her parents had been able to emigrate from Earth, she could live on this alien ground. But her parents had come to a place prepared for them. There were already fifty million people settled on Zarathustra. First one island, then a chain, had been sterilized and terraformed by experts, assessing the risk from native life-forms, whether they were useful, neutral, or dangerous. A complete new ecology had been designed to include domestic creatures, plants, even bacteria brought from Earth, and only after half a century's careful organization were immigrants invited, with one of the fabulous human computers called "polymaths" to supervise and protect them.

What chance did a few hundred refugees, with hardly any tools or weapons, a handful of scientists, and no experience of existence at such a primitive level, stand in face of a hostile and unpredictable world?

"Ornelle! Ornelle!"

With a guilty start she raised her head. Standing in the rough doorway, one hand holding aside the curtain and the other carrying his medikit, was Doc Jerode. His white shirt and overfoot breeches were yellowing and frayed, and since being out of reach of tricholene treatments his mass of shining gray hair had thinned to a crescent on the back of his head. But he was picking up a healthy-looking tan.

"I'm sorry, Doc. Didn't hear you come in." Ornelle licked her lips. Her throat was stiff after her fit of sobbing, and the words came painfully. "I'm all right. Just a bit tired."

"Tired!" the doctor said. "Exhausted is more the word."

He strode forward, his feet noisy on the crude planks of the floor, and set his medikit on the table. "Here, I'm going to make sure you haven't picked up an infection. Get your clothes off."

"Oh—oh, very well." Ornelle rose to her feet and unfastened her shirt. Like everyone else, she had been stifled throughout the winter by the sensation of having all possible clothing on against the cold, that daily grew greasier and fouler-smelling, and now was wearing only outer garments. She stood slackly as Jerode ran his diagnoser over her.

"Nothing on the culture slide except bugs I recognize," he said at last. He surveyed her curiously. "So you're right. You're simply worn out. But . . . how long have you been at that radio?"

"Uh . . . most of the past three days," she admitted.

"Have you slept properly? Don't answer that—I can tell you haven't. And I've watched you gulping your meals in your hurry to get back here. Take one of these." Jerode selected a tube of small white pills from his kit, giving a rueful glance at how few of them remained. "Blast you, woman! Why do you have to let me down?"

"What?" Ornelle had a mug of water on the table; she checked in the act of reaching for it to wash down the pill.

"You heard me. Here I've been telling myself that you are one of the reliable people we have, able to think fairly straight in spite of being completely unprepared for this predicament, while so many who are supposed to be trained or talented have taken to running around in circles gibbering! But, like I say, you're letting me down."

"I don't understand," Ornelle muttered.

"To start with, what's the panic about contacting the other party? They probably had a far tougher winter on high ground. Our antenna collapsed. So may theirs have, and it might still be buried in a snowdrift. Even if they have had time to worry about setting it up again, they may not have anyone to spare to sit by a radio and hope to hear from us. Give them a chance to clear up the mess of winter and get themselves organized."

"If they were in bad trouble," Ornelle said stonily, "the first thing they'd want to know would be if we're OK. If they weren't in trouble, then they'd want to find out if we were and needed any help. No, I'm afraid there's not much hope for them." She sighed and gulped down the pill.

"So that's the weight you've got on your shoulders. An imaginary one. I thought so."

"Weight on my shoulders? What do you mean?"

"You're standing there like a—a badly stuffed doll! Here, look at yourself." Jerode unfolded the lid of his medikit and snapped it to the mirror setting. "You ought to be ashamed of maltreating your body that way."

Dully, Ornelle regarded her reflection. Her skin was pallid, there was a slackness around her eyes as well as the red of tiredness and tears, and her breasts, pale-nippled, were like shrunken pears. Whereas her belly was sagging forward.

Not from fat.

"Pull it in, woman," Jerode ordered. "Take a deep breath, set your shoulders back, and look at the improvement."

He waited while she obeyed. Then, as he saw a change of expression pass across her face, he shut the kit.

"You need some sun," he said. "Ten or fifteen minutes a day for the first few days, no more—I'm troubled enough with sunburn cases. But I want a color on you like mine in ten days, understand? All over. You don't get much calciferol from sunlight, but we've got to take advantage of everything."

Flushing, Ornelle turned to pick up her clothes from the chair where she had hung them. "I'm sorry," she said after a while. "It's just—oh, you know."

Jerode didn't say anything. She went on, "Anyway, what did you want me for?"

"A bit of advice. I need a woman's opinion before I make up my mind on a problem that's just arisen. You know Delvia?"

Drawing her shirt on, Ornelle gave a bitter chuckle. "Do I know that—that exhibitionist? Does anyone not?"

"Yes, she is rather atypical of our group, isn't she? Conspicuous! Well, she came to see me—one of the sunburn cases I mentioned—and I checked her over. She's pregnant."

Ornelle stared blankly. "Well, I'd never have expected that," she said at length.

"Why? Because she's not the maternal type?"

"That she's not! No, I wouldn't have expected her to be so careless. It's not that she lacks experience, I'll swear to that. In fact . . ." Ornelle hesitated. "In fact I think she's downright nymphomaniac."

"Is it true that you've had trouble with her in the single women's house?"

"Who told you that?"

"People tell doctors things, don't they? And since we don't have a psychologist . . . That's irrelevant, anyway. The point is this. We agreed collectively on arrival that we weren't going to permit children until we knew more about our environment. Embryonic tissue is fragile, and we don't want to start off with teratoid births. That was a unanimous decision on my advice. I think we'll probably be safe in relaxing the rule now—in fact, I planned to ask for volunteer parents at the stocktaking assembly tomorrow. But it still stands at the moment. And, as you agree, Delvia is not the sort of person who'd be suitable. We can't have people flouting our collective decisions, can we?"

"Of course not."

"So I've been wondering whether we oughtn't to establish a precedent by imposing a compulsory abortion on her."

Ornelle was silent for a moment. "Are you asking for my personal opinion?" she said eventually. "Or are you asking what the reaction of the other women is likely to be?"

"Both."

"Well . . . I think most of us would agree that you can't have people disregarding the rules, and particularly since Delvia is—uh—not too popular, you'd have no trouble getting such a motion carried."

"Speaking for yourself, though?"

Ornelle closed her eyes. "If our stay here is likely to be for good, I'd hate to think it had been marred by that sort of thing right at the start. Besides, that was one of the things that made the winter so intolerable: losing the babies. Having children around is part of life for me—an indispensable part. And since you say you were planning to recommend starting some pregnancies . . ."

"Yes." Jerode rubbed his chin. "If this were anyone but Delvia I'd be inclined to overlook it. I still could. I doubt if she knows herself yet; it's only five or six days gone. But, as you say, she must have been careless, or else she was defying a rule she doesn't approve of. Both are dangerous trends, aren't they? Especially in such a forceful personality."

"A compulsory abortion, though . . . I'll have to think about it, I'm afraid."

"Please do. We're having a preliminary committee meeting at dark this evening. I'd like you to come to it and tell us your conclusions, all right?"

"Yes, of course." And she added as he turned to the door: "Doc, did you have children—back home?"

"Yes. And I know you did too. Which is why I came to consult you."

◆ IV ◆

Lex slipped into the water, feeling extraordinarily distant from it because the spacesuit he was wearing insulated him so efficiently. To be in water without feeling its coolness was disconcerting. He hadn't remarked the fact during the dives he had done last year, but his mind had been taken up by other things. He had been searching for Bendle's son; on the first dive he had found him, on the second recovered the body—or rather, what was left of it. It had been no consolation at all to see that the hungry marine beasts which had nibbled at his flesh were still clinging, discolored and dying, because some compound in human protoplasm was poisoning them.

He drew a deep breath, conscious that thinking such morbid thoughts would handicap the speed of his reactions, and caught at the anchor cable so that he could pause before reaching the bottom and take proper stock of his surroundings.

The silver egg-form of the ship seemed to be about one-third buried. The seabed, for a considerable distance from shore, was composed of the same relatively firm greenish sand as the beach, but out here it was slack and muddy, carpeted with a mass of juicy weed, and the hull had sunk deep. In the wan, diffuse light he could not tell whether the occasional movements he detected among the fronded aquatic plants were due to currents, or whether animal-life was hiding among the branches.

There were no openings to the ship except the locks: two for the crew, two much larger ones for cargo. He could just discern the top on an open cargo lock on this side of the hull, above the level of the vegetation. That was fortunate. He could enter through there and probably conduct quite an extensive exploration, though sand and mud would doubtless have sifted over much of the gear inside.

For a moment a stab of anger against fate made him clench his teeth. As though it weren't bad enough to be stranded on an unknown planet with only the basic resources of a space-freighter and some odds and ends crammed hastily aboard before their takeoff: now much of even that scanty material was out here, spoiled by a winter's immersion. What they had removed from the ship had been dictated by immediate necessity. They had taken out conventional radio equipment, for instance, because they had foreseen the need to keep in touch with exploring parties even before the question of the other refugees arose.

But what use was conventional radio when they wanted to broadcast their whereabouts across the interstellar gulf? For that, you needed the ship's subradios. And those had not been taken out for two good reasons: first, the attenuation factor, and second, their appetite for power. Subradio was virtually instantaneous over parsec distances, but it was almost nullified by the blanket of a planetary atmosphere. When calling planet-to-planet it was necessary to relay your message with conventional radio to an orbiting satellite where the signal was automatically converted. And in any case you had to bleed power from the ship's fusion drive in order to kick your beam between the stars.

If only, before landing, they had been able to leave a subradio beacon in orbit. . . . They had broadcast constantly during the flight, of course, but they were almost outrunning their own signals, and by the time they arrived in this system they were half choking with CO_2 and anthropotoxins. The ship's air-purifiers hadn't been meant to cope with eight hundred people. They had to land at once.

Maybe it didn't matter anyhow. They were at least twenty parsecs beyond the limit of previous exploration.

Maybe no one would have thought to watch for signals from so far out.

Hence the subradios had been left in the ship. Hence they were at the bottom of the sea and more than likely corroded past repair. Diet-synthesizers, tools, accumulators, solar energy collectors, medical equipment, books, tapes, scientific instruments—what few there were—had been taken inland. But very little else.

Lex sighed and made to continue his descent. It seemed, when he looked about him, that the water was darker. A cloud crossing the sun? It wasn't likely; the sky had been clear a few minutes ago. He snapped on his handlight and found that didn't help. His vision was blurred. But why?

He spent a short while puzzling out what had happened. Then the glass lens of the handlight gave him the clue. It was coated with a thin greenish film, which easily rubbed off. So was his helmet. In fact the entire surface of his suit was sliming completely over with what he judged to be the local equivalent of plankton. That hadn't happened on his dives last year—but of course summer had been nearly over, and no doubt spring brought an exuberance of new life.

He didn't imagine it would prove dangerous, just inconvenient. Playing the handlight on the ship's hull, he saw that the bright metal was only misted, implying that the stuff did not build up layer by layer.

Hooking the light to its helmet mount so that he would not have to release his grip on the cable, he detached a couple of the rocks which weighted his belt. Neutral buoyancy would be better under these conditions than any weight at all. He didn't like the look of the massed vegetation around the lower edge of the open cargo lock, and wanted to see if he could drift or swim into the ship without touching the plants.

Something brushed the hand with which he was grasping the cable.

His head and light turned together. Revealed was a reddish creature with many claw-tipped feet and a baglike body from which fronds like those of the bottom-weed swirled gracefully. It was walking up the cable, holding tight with groups of four claws, and on coming to the obstacle, his hand, had paused to investigate. A leechlike neck with a ring of antennae fringing a dark sucking mouth was fumbling along his arm.

The light seemed not to affect it at all. Eyes were

developing extraordinarily late among these sea-beasts, Bendle had said, although many of them had patches of skin responsive to light and dark.

It might not be able to harm him, Lex thought. But those claws looked unpleasantly powerful. Besides, it would not be good for Aldric and Cheffy to find this thing swarming up into the boat. It was about four feet long, and a nip or bite from it might be as poisonous to man as human flesh apparently was to the local creatures.

He readied his hatchet. Then, as the beast decided his arm offered a better course than continuing up the cable, he swung the blade and severed the first six or eight of its clawed legs, expecting it to fall.

Instantly, the fronded bag at the rear of the creature burst open and the water turned a filthy yellow color which blinded him completely within seconds. Startled, Lex lost his grip on the cable and began to fall toward the bottom.

As soon as he was out of the yellow cloud, he twisted around and saw it from a few yards away, a misshapen ball. Out of it, like darts, plunged a score or more of stiff, wriggling-legged miniatures of the thing he had attacked. All of them were heading toward him. He flailed the hatchet violently, beating them off as he tumbled in the water, but two of them attached themselves to his faceplate. He saw how their little leech-mouths opened wide, spread to a diameter of two inches, began to fold back as if the creatures were going to turn completely inside-out.

His feet found bottom. He straightened and clawed the creatures loose, hurling them from him as far as the resistance of the water would allow. By this time the mouths had folded back halfway along the bodies and the capacity to swim seemed to have been lost altogether. The things dropped among the weed and something— Lex couldn't tell what because it moved so fast—engulfed them, emitting a moment later a jet of the ubiquitous yellow ink.

Lex was beginning to regret his offhand decision to make this trip alone. He had never imagined such a totally unwelcoming environment. He had told himself many times during the past winter that now it was up to man to prove himself superior to the competing lifeforms by being a more efficient animal. But here for the first time he was beginning to appreciate what the truism really implied.

He was standing a few yards from the cargo lock, swaying because he had made himself too light for stability yet not light enough to float. The compromise might be satisfactory if it enabled him to make slow leaps like a man in barely perceptible gravity. His legs were calf-deep in the bottom-weed and his boot-soles apparently in squelchy mud, but he didn't seem to be sinking in.

Something passed between him and the gleaming roof of the surface. He glanced up and saw a pulsing creature with a flat planelike body and clusters of irregularly-distributed tentacles dangling beneath. It took no notice of him. Several other creatures, large and small, were likewise pursuing their own affairs overhead.

Well, if they ignored him, he'd ignore them. He aimed himself at the cargo lock. A carefully-judged leap, dreamlike in the water, brought him with a slight bump against the upper left corner of the opening where he could grip a projection and look inside.

All the time he had spent here, in crudely-rigged metal-framed bunks hard as tables, came back to memory. This had been the hold in which four hundred men had been crammed for the voyage. Sand had sifted across the tilted floor, and patching it now were weeds and little round sessile animals with fernlike filter-mouths which sorted drifting plankton from the water. On the walls clung sucker-rooted colonies of symbiotic cell-associations, vaguely similar to stranded algae.

Already the ship was becoming a water-jungle. Lex knew at that first glance that salvage operations were going to take much of this long summer, and at that it was a toss-up whether power-tools could be brought down to reclaim the valuable metals from the hull itself.

Since the sand-floor was relatively clear, he pushed himself down to it and ventured a little farther into the ship. Fortunately, a few of the internal doors were still closed. Strange animals, lost in the corridors, scuttered at his approach or adopted stiff threatening postures which he might have found ludicrous but that on this planet he had no standard yet by which to judge such matters. He made his way along the spinal tunnel of the ship, not wanting to open any sealed doors in case they were still airtight, toward the forward control sections.

Here were the most precious items. And here the chaos was terrible.

Computers, loosed from their mounts in readiness for transfer to the town, then left behind when winter intervened, had fallen across the floor and been shattered. The subradios were—as he had feared—corroded and crusted with crystals of sea-salt. The navigation room was a shambles out of which he could pick nothing but a few odds and ends to drop in his net bag.

Depressed, he made his way toward the stern, where the engines were located. Something bad had happened here, too; a gap big enough to walk through in the wall of the fuel-reserve store was the first sign of a succession of chemical explosions that had wrecked most of the drive gear beyond repair. His light revealed smears of multi-colored corrosion, cracked plates, instrument panels pock-marked as though by shrapnel.

He could sum up his report for tomorrow's stocktaking assembly here and now. Nothing in the ship worth salvaging except as raw materials.

Oh, perhaps the odd instrument might be reparable and come in handy for some unpredictable function. But nothing as immediately useful as power-tools or accumulators could have survived.

Scraping the latest film of green from his helmet, he turned dejectedly back the way he had come.

His first thought when he approached the cargo lock from inside was that the sea had gone dark. Then he saw that the opening was blocked by something. His light showed a slick dark surface, pulsating and straining, splitting open along horizontal lines to emit hordes of tiny flapping things toward which the hanging strands on the walls reached out eagerly.

At the sight of this, a tremendous anger filled him. He spoke aloud, hearing the words echo eerie in his helmet.

"Damn you! It's still ours! In spite of everything, it's still *ours!*"

He raised his hatchet and stormed forward at the creature sowing its multitudinous young. They swarmed like midges around him as he chopped, ripped, tore at the leathery flesh, with his hand as well as the hatchet; plunged through the very middle of it, through writhing blackness and out into discolored water where hopeful lesser carnivores were already gathering to pick at car-

rion; then, covered with foul ichor and trailing some
riband-formed internal organ of the beast, in dismal tri-
umph to the surface and the boat, leaving the shabby
symbol of his defiance to die on the bed of the sea.

◆ V ◆

Zarathustra's day had run about twenty-two and a half
hours Earth-basic time and, as was customary on colo-
nized planets, had been cut into an arbitrary standard
twenty hours. Here on the other hand noon-to-noon ran
about twenty-eight Earth basic hours. Some attempt had
been made to modify one of the clocks from the ship, but
there had been more demanding tasks. Now clocks and
natural time were totally out of gear, though a record
was being kept of the number of days elapsed.

Was it a matter of mere convenience that people were
suddenly thinking in terms of daylight and dark, or the
first sign of reversion to actual primitivism? Jerode pondered the question as he looked out over their ramshackle
little town from the crude verandah of the headquarters
office. Most people were coming for evening chow, walking slowly and wearily back from their work, although
Fritch's team was still busy patching the roof of the single men's house the other side of the valley. The thud
of hammers and an occasional shouted order reached
his ears.

He had already had his meal, wanting a little time to
think before the steering committee assembled at dusk.
It had consisted as usual of a damp mealy cake from
a diet-synthesizer wrapped in two crisp leaflike growths
from the salad-tree and a chunk of preserved allfruit
about the size of his thumb. So far only the salad-tree
and three other much less palatable native plants had
been found both safe and nutritious. Most of the vegetation contained an allergen which had given him a bad
time at the end of last summer until he discovered he
had supplies of a suitable drug with which to treat it.

Like everybody else, when leaving Zarathustra he had simply grabbed what he could lay hands on, and wasn't sure what he'd actually brought.

That, though, was going to have to change. As a matter of urgency they would be compelled to tinker with one of the synthesizers so that it would secrete an antidote to the allergen. Dredged routinely on food, perhaps along with sea-salt, it would enable them to choose from a range of nearly thirty vegetables.

And the trace-element hoppers on the synthesizers were almost empty—during the worst part of the winter they had had to subsist on nothing but synthesizer-cake —so another immediate job would be to set up extra salt-pans, fractionate the precipitate into appropriate submixtures, top the hoppers up . . .

Jerode passed a tired hand over his face. There was no end to the list of essential tasks.

There was a steady stream away from the kitchens as well as toward them, which seemed odd; he saw people coming out directly they had entered. Then he realized they were taking their food to the riverbank, to sit there and eat in the last of the sunlight with their long shadows for company. Well, at least the evening sun wouldn't cause much burning. And you couldn't blame them. The equable, man-controlled climate of Zarathrustra had delivered warm summer evenings to order, and after the dragging-long winter to be under a roof seemed like a waste.

That river was a blessing, Jerode thought. It wasn't very wide except at the mouth, and it was shallow enough for wading even now, when the snows must be melting around its source on the plateau inland. Of course, it had divided the settlement during the worst nights of winter, but they had just managed to rig a ropewalk across it before the fiercest gales, and that had been strong enough to hold out. Siting the town on both banks, though, had been a calculated risk. They didn't want to drag timber too far, and there were two stands of trees they were drawing on, one either side of the valley.

Most importantly of all, they had never lacked drinkable fresh water, even if they had sometimes had to bring it indoors as blocks of ice. Though it might be politic, once enough salt-pans had been set up, to use distilled water for drinking, reserve river-water only for bathing in . . .

Yes, considering the circumstances of its foundation, this was quite a flourishing little town. Town? Well, it wasn't such a grandiose word as "city," at least. But for a mere fifteen buildings it was still a pious hope. At first they had slept in the ship, but the cramped quarters were inducing fearful tension among the refugees. He himself had insisted that an early start be made on housing. So they had found dense clay along the river, spread it to make floors, and set up long one-story buildings, using split-log planks on a frame of natural tree-posts, and Lex, who was clever at such things, had helped him doctor a diet-synthesizer to secrete a tough organic glue which had endured—most of it—through the winter. A barracks for single men, another for single women, five others divided crudely into screened-off cubicles for couples who had either been together when the evacuation started or linked up aboard ship for mutual comfort.

There had been problems when new attachments formed during the winter, of course. But the few fights could be ascribed to anxiety and claustrophobia. The traditions of Zarathustra, like most well-settled colony planets, had been opposed to violent sexual jealousy. And plans were in hand for extending the—well, the married accommodation.

Jerode sighed. Yes, there was going to have to be some kind of discipline to make these ad hoc unions stick, something stiffer than the casual suit-yourself practices of Zarathustra. Because there would be children this year if the assembly agreed, and children must *not* become a community charge. There would be too much resentment from nonparents.

He wished he knew more about primitive psychology. He had picked up a few pointers from Cheffy, but basically their social evolution would have to be a cut-and-try process, like everything else.

Four of the original fifteen houses were currently derelict. They had been incomplete at the start of the winter, and cannibalized by Fritch to reinforce the walls of the bigger buildings. This one, the headquarters hut which served as a kind of administrative office, was in fairly good shape, though. Jerode gave the split-log planks of the wall an approving nudge.

His mere touch dislodged one of the planks. It fell with a crash.

Heart sinking, he bent to examine it. On the brownish

smear of glue which had held it in place, a cluster of yellow specks moved uncertainly, as though startled by the sudden light. Some parasite which had found the glue digestible. Add one to the list of immediate jobs.

"I see you've discovered our latest problem, Doc," a voice said from behind him. He turned. It was Fritch, the burly dark-brown man who had been an architect on Zarathustra and had supervised all their building here.

"You have a lot of it? Is it serious?" Jerode demanded.

"Pretty." Fritch shrugged. He was holding his evening meal sandwich-wise in one hand, and had been biting at it as he walked. "Little Hannet leaned on a plank where that mold or whatever had been at work, and it gave way and she fell ten feet. Wasn't hurt, luckily. Landed on a bed."

"So are all our houses going to collapse on our heads?"

"No, I don't think so. I've put a team to work cutting nails out of scrap sheet metal. We can reinforce the worst-affected walls until you or Bendle find something to mix with the glue and make it unpalatable. Bendle says he thinks there's antimony in some of the sea-plants, and we can burn a sample and see if adding the ash helps. Anyway," he concluded, raising his food to his mouth again, "I see I needn't have hurried over. I thought I'd find everyone else here."

"Arbogast is coming," Jerode said, looking toward the river. "Bendle is back from the beach, and so are Aldric and Cheffy—saw them go for chow a few minutes ago. Did you see Lex?"

"Yes. He managed to get inside the ship. Says it's in hopeless condition."

"We weren't expecting much. Still," Jerode amended, frowning, "if Lex says it's bad we can take it literally. If Arbogast had said it, I'd have assumed he was disheartened. What did he say, do you know? Did he concur?"

"He didn't go down." Fritch spoke around a mouthful.

"Didn't he?" Jerode exclaimed. "Why?"

"I gather he couldn't face it."

"I don't like the sound of that," Jerode muttered. "I think I'd better have a private word with him later."

"You're not going to like the sound of this either," Fritch said. "Nanseltine is agitating for membership of the steering committee, and a lot of people have fallen for his argument that someone who was a full continental manager back home must necessarily be competent for the job."

"He isn't." Jerode's tone was final. "Someone who did nothing the whole winter long but sit on his butt and complain simply doesn't have what it takes."

"Sure, I agree. But I'm afraid you're going to have to face a lot of opposition tomorrow."

There was silence for a moment. Then Arbogast came in sight around the corner of the adjacent hut, walking with head bowed. When they greeted him he muttered his reply and went straight inside to take his place at the committee table.

Jerode lifted an eyebrow at Fritch, who shrugged.

"You'll just have to do what you can to straighten him out, Doc," he murmured. "We're so short of capable people."

Jerode nodded and answered equally softly: "I asked Ornelle to attend the meeting, by the way. I've always pegged her as basically sensible, and I gather she's become the de facto administrator in the single women's house. We're going to need people to take care of human problems now, as well as simply organizing the work we have to do."

"Not a bad idea," Fritch approved. "But the person I'm really pinning my hopes on is young Lex. He's the most original mind we have. The rest of us—well, let's face it. We're shackled by the preconceptions we brought from home. He's naturally inventive, isn't he?"

"Quiet," Jerode said. "Here he comes."

A few minutes later they were all assembled around the rough table: Arbogast at the head by custom, Jerode on his right. Since, during the voyage here, everyone had grown used to obeying their captain, relying on their doctor, it had been automatic to let them remain in charge. Then came Fritch, Bendle, Aldric, Cheffy, self-elected for their specialist knowledge or professional skills. Bendle looked terribly tired. Then Ornelle, subdued and wan, and last, facing Arbogast, Lex, who had been co-opted when he proposed the ropewalk over the river, and since then had come up with several suggestions for improvised gadgetry that surprised even Cheffy, with his extensive grounding in early human history.

No, Nanseltine wouldn't fit in, Jerode thought. *That's our justification for being here. We work well together.*

*He's a man accustomed to giving orders, nothing else.
And he's not even a competent planner, really, just a
mouthpiece for computers of the kind we don't have.*

But it had worried him that no woman had emerged
who was an obvious choice for a position of authority
like the rest of them. Thinking ahead to the days when
there might be time for petty politics, when the single
women would be a pressure group to reckon with, he had
hit on Ornelle, because—as he had told Fritch—she had
become a kind of housemother figure. He was not, though,
entirely sure she was a good choice.

Still, time would tell.

He waited. There was silence. They looked expectantly
at Arbogast, who had his hands on the table palms up,
the fingers curled over. He didn't raise his head.

In a grating voice he said suddenly, "I—I think I
should vacate this place in favor of someone who deserves it."

He thrust back his chair with a scraping noise and
walked out, looking neither right nor left.

Bendle and Ornelle, astonished, made to stop him.
Jerode and Fritch exchanged glances and signaled to the
others not to speak. When Arbogast was gone, Jerode
made up his mind. He moved to the head of the table
and cleared his throat.

"I'm afraid the captain is unwell," he said. "He's been
much affected by—well, by what's become of his ship.
You know about this already, I think?"

Nods from Lex, Aldric, Cheffy, Fritch. Jerode glanced
down at notes he had made, spread on the table before
him.

"So I'll have a quiet talk with him later. For now, let's
not discuss it, but get straight down to business. I'll report on the health situation, then we'll hear from Lex
regarding the ship, Fritch about accommodation, Bendle
about our summer biosphere, Aldric about material resources, Cheffy about possible new projects. Then we'll
draw up a priorities list, and before we adjourn I think
we'd better—uh—spend a little time on a problem which
is going to come up at the assembly tomorrow, which is
the reason for my asking Ornelle to join us. Right!"

It wasn't too bad. It wasn't too bad at all. When they
had run through all the reports and the list was complete
but for some undecided questions concerning relative ur-

gency, Jerode judged they were ready to hear his recommendation, not included in his initial statement, about permitting some experimental births. He added the rider that the permission should be limited to the immediate future so that children now conceived would be delivered before the fall.

"And that brings us to a special problem of group discipline," he wound up. Warning them that the matter should not be mentioned outside this room, he explained about Delvia.

All of them looked to Ornelle for comment. She had not previously spoken.

"As to the question of children," she said slowly, "I think we've got to say yes. Not only because it may help to give us the psychological roots we'll need to live here . . ."

A good point. Approving nods.

"But also because there were few enough of us to start with, and now the winter has wiped out the other party—"

"Ornelle!" Jerode cut in, seeing dismayed looks all around the table. "There's no proof that the others haven't survived."

"Well, nobody said anything at this meeting about sending an expedition to find out!" Ornelle retorted. "That means you're taking it for granted, doesn't it?"

"Of course not," Jerode soothed. "It's because we need all our manpower until we've coped with our really urgent problems."

"Nonsense. If anyone here believed they were alive, you'd be eager to get up to the plateau and see if we can help each other." Ornelle spoke with finality. "Anyway, I don't see why we need to argue about Delvia. I've been mulling the question over, and I'm damned certain there's no question of imposing an abortion on her. She's much more likely to come asking you for one. She'd find a child too much of a handicap on her—her other activities. Believe me. I've had the whole winter to watch her at close quarters, you know."

"That's as may be," Jerode said. "What I'm worried about is the risk that if the news gets around, there may be still more resentment against her, because we didn't enforce what was, after all, a decision taken collectively by us all."

"Oh, sure!" Ornelle leaned forward, elbows on the table. "But there's something that doesn't seem to have occurred to all you men. It wasn't conscious choice that led all the women to agree to a ban on babies. It was despair. Apathy. The belief that there wasn't any *point* in having children, because we were all quite likely to die, adults, children, the lot. All right, you're now about to convince everybody that we aren't doomed, what with your nice tidy plans that you've been discussing. So you've got to face this brand-new problem!" She slapped the table. "What are you going to do, once you've made people confident, if they decide—collectively!—they're no longer going to do exactly as you self-appointed experts tell them?"

◆ VI ◆

"I'm glad you thought of inviting Ornelle," Lex said in a low voice. Jerode glanced up from shuffling his notes back into their original order. The substance they were written on had been their first fortunate discovery here; there was a river-plant whose leaves grew in tight yellow scrolls which, unrolled, could be dried and trimmed to make an excellent substitute for paper. Though they did stink for a long while after cutting.

The others were already at the door. Ornelle herself was outside, beyond earshot. Nonetheless Jerode replied equally softly.

"Why do you think it was a good idea? She hasn't been a very constructive contributor, and I'm revising my opinion of her."

"No, it was useful having her here." Lex perched himself on a corner of the table, one long leg swinging from the knee, his lean face serious under his roughly-trimmed dark hair. "Know what the trouble is with most of our people, Doc?"

"Tell me your diagnosis," Jerode invited sourly.

"Remoteness from reality," Lex said, unperturbed. "Not in any clinical sense, I don't mean—not in the form of an overt psychological disorder. It's a straightforward consequence of the way we're used to living." He leaned forward a little.

"Consider how detached most of us have always been from the necessities of life. Zara wasn't a very wealthy planet; even so, it kept ticking along fine with its people putting in something like five hours a day four days a week in technical, managerial, supervisory tasks. And at that Zarathustrans worked harder than a lot of other people. Suppose we were from Earth, for example, where you're absolutely free to opt for total leisure—where there's so much available that it literally makes no difference whether any given person does any work.

"Now look at those of us who've had responsibility devolve on us. What do we have in common? Nothing, as far as I can judge, except flexibility. We've adjusted more rapidly than the rest, and in each case you can see why. Fritch, a creative person used to seeing his ideas turned into hardware, willing if all else fails to use his own hands to make sure that goes on being true. Bendle, a research scientist who can let his lifelong interest in new flora and fauna drive him day after day. Cheffy, an amateur historian who has at least some comprehension of what life must be like if you don't have automated factories all around you. Aldric, a model-maker, a craftsman born out of his time. And you, used to working on other people's behalf. No, don't deny it. Now you're stuck with the job Arbogast couldn't handle, and modesty is going to be a handicap."

Jerode studied Lex thoughtfully. This was an aspect of the younger man he hadn't previously encountered. He said, "Curiously enough I was thinking about that just before the meeting."

"Not in connection with Nanseltine, by any chance?"

"Yes. How did you guess?"

"Didn't guess. Smelled it coming, you might say. That's why I said I'm glad Ornelle came along tonight. Because she's typical of our human resources. You aren't. Fritch isn't. But I'm afraid Nanseltine is absolutely archetypal."

"I hope you're very wrong," Jerode said after a pause. "All I've heard from him lately—or from his wife, come to that—is a stream of complaints disguised as helpful criticism, and a lot of hypochondriacal disease symptoms. How he ever held down his continental manager's post, I shall never know." He hesitated.

"But, speaking of the reasons for us winding up as

members of the committee: how about you? If you dis-
approve of people being modest, I guess that entitles me
to tell you that you possess the most original mind among
us all. Item: you said you had no training for space, but
when it turned out that that crewman had gone on ground-
leave and not come back, you were the one who served
as scratch crew, right? And I don't recall any complaints
from Arbogast. And you hit on the ropewalk, and I think
it was you who realized we could adapt a spacesuit to dive
in search of young Bendle, and—well, and so on. Now it's
got to the point where, if we hit a snag, we're likely to
go ask you for a solution instead of puzzling one out ourselves. Yet I realize I know practically nothing about you."

Lex laughed and rose to his feet, stretching. "Well, Doc,
that's not surprising. We were almost all total strangers,
weren't we? We just got thrown together."

"I think I might have a straight answer." Jerode looked
the younger man in the eyes. He had to tip his head back
to do so. "You've explained why Fritch and Bendle and
the rest of us are fitted to cope here. I've just explained
why you are. But—well, it can't be nothing more than
lack of ingrained prejudice about the way the universe
ought to function! How old are you, anyway?"

Lex hesitated. He said finally, "Twenty, Earth-basic
years."

"What?" Jerode took a pace backward. "Now look here,
Lex! I'm medically trained, and I say twenty's ridiculous.
You're a biological thirty in exceptional shape, give or
take a year!"

"No, in fact I'm not." Lex seemed oddly embarrassed.
"That's—uh—protective coloration. You see, I'm a trainee
polymath. Tetraploid genes, modified neurons, vision extended into the infrared, heightened reflexes, accelerated
nerve-signal transmission, compacted bone structure, in-
duced immunity to more or less everything. . . . Oh, they
gave me the full treatment. But I can't take credit for any
of it. It was all done for me."

Jerode's mouth had fallen unashamedly open. Now he
realized and snapped it shut. "A *polymath*!" he exploded.
"Why in all of space didn't you say so before?"

"Because when I say trainee I mean trainee." Lex's
voice was level but sharp. "Have you any idea how far I
was from completing my studies? Of course you haven't.
Longer than I've lived up to now! It takes a quarter-
century to make a finished polymath. If Arbogast hadn't

moved out of that chair tonight, I wouldn't have told you. And I don't want you to tell anybody else."

"No! No, you can't say that." Jerode was sweating; the single lamp which they'd lighted at sunset gleamed on his face. "Lex, of all the people here you're the only one who's been given any kind of preparation for a situation like ours. That means you're the one best fitted for overall responsibility. Like it or not, you're better fitted than I am, anyhow!"

"Think again," Lex said stonily. "Think why I was given an appearance ten years over my chronological age. You, and all the rest, are thinking of me nonetheless as 'young Lex.' How old are you, Doc? Seventy?"

"Sixty-nine."

"And a long way from old. Average life-expectancy on Zara is—was—one hundred twelve for men, one hundred eighteen for women. What's it going to be around here, without geriatric clinics, tissue regenerants, orthophased diets—not to mention *with* all kinds of as-yet undetermined deficiencies, allergies, maybe infections? In one generation it'll be cut by three-quarters at least, and someone your age will be a remarkable old man! But right now none of the older people, least of all those who used to possess rank on Zara, will accept orders from a mere 'youngster.' You know that! And one more thing!" He poked a finger toward Jerode.

"A polymath is trained to take charge of a newly opened planet. *One particular planet.* He doesn't even move to it until he's past forty. He's not left in sole charge until he's sixty. At ninety he's usually retired because the job has been done. Very often he dies a few years later, burned out. But satisfied. Because he's had a lifelong love affair with an entire planet, something no conceivable human relationship could match. He's known it more intimately than most husbands ever get to know their wives."

He moved toward the door, a shadow approaching deeper shadow outside. On the threshold he glanced back for a moment.

"Which may explain to you the most important thing. This is not *my* world. I don't *want* the job."

Outside, the alien star-patterns loomed out of soft velvet sky. Moodily Lex walked toward the single men's house, from which drifted the sound of laughter. But he had only gone a few yards when he heard his name spoken, and he turned to find Ornelle standing there uncertainly, hands linked before her.

"Do you mind walking down the hill with me?" she said in a low voice. "I—I was wanting to ask you a favor. I don't want to seem to be meddling in other people's affairs, but I think someone's got to take responsibility, and . . . and, to be honest, after sitting through your committee meeting, I find everyone else in the bunch presumptuous and bossy."

Lex sighed, knowing the sound was too faint to be heard, and said politely, "Well, if there's anything I can do to help . . ."

She fell in beside him, not looking at him. "It was talking about Delvia that made up my mind for me," she said. "You know Naline?"

"Of course. Not very well."

"What do you think of her?"

Lex pondered for a moment, wondering what this was leading up to. He said, "Frankly, she hasn't made much impression on me. She's probably shy by nature, though she does overcompensate by sometimes being brash. Unsure of herself, badly upset like the rest of us with less adult experience to help stabilize her—she's only sixteen, isn't she? But she's above average intelligence. She'll make out."

"Attractive?"

Now why ask that? Lex's interest began to quicken. In fact, she was rather plain, with a characterless round face and a figure which, though hunger had melted off the puppy-fat, was nothing to remark on. Her long dark hair was her best feature, but she'd said something today about cutting it off.

He compromised. "I guess maybe not very, if you're judging by the standards of Zara. But standards are going to change, and change fast, under these conditions."

Ornelle halted. They had come to the riverbank at the spot where she had to turn toward the single women's house. Now she turned and faced him.

"Look, Lex. I'll be blunt. Naline isn't pretty. She is young, but that won't last. And I . . . well, I had twin daughters at home, not as old as her, but nearly. And there's Delvia, who doesn't care much about other people. She uses them. Luckily most adults know how to prevent that happening. Naline doesn't."

"I still don't see," Lex murmured. In fact he was starting to suspect what she was referring to, but he wanted her to spell it out.

"I've tried to keep things quiet," Ornelle said. "I didn't want to cause any worse rows in that claustrophobic place than we've been enduring all along." A gesture toward the women's house. "And Del does have some good traits; she's a capable person, and she certainly has vitality, though she's very coarse and insensitive with it. So Naline must have been flattered when Del took to courting her."

"You mean that literally?"

"Can you imagine Del settling for half-measures? Oh, she isn't the only one! I mean, one realizes it's part of human nature, and all of us being cooped up together like that. . . . But for Del it's nothing more than a stopgap." She caught herself, then gave a sour chuckle. "Yes, that's a very apt term! She does have some signs of a conscience, I must admit. I mean, she hasn't just thrown Naline aside now the winter's over and there's a chance to sneak off in the woods with men again. But Naline is just clinging on by a hair now, and sooner or later she's going to have a terrible shock when Del starts parading around with a man she prefers."

Frowning, Lex said, "You don't think she's found him already?"

"Her pregnancy? Oh, she's probably been dragging the nearest man up the hill twice a day since it got warm enough to lie down without frostbite. Trying all of them in turn."

It crossed Lex's mind that if that were true then Delvia was making a better adjustment to the realities of their new home than Ornelle, or indeed practically anybody else.

"Well, you've explained the problem," he said. "But I don't see what I can do."

"Don't you?" Ornelle moved closer and put her hand on his arm. "Lex, I don't think I could ask any other of the single men to do it, but you seem more self-possessed and sensible than the rest of them. Somebody's got to cushion the shock for Naline. At that age she doesn't have fully-developed emotions—she's still at the hero-worship stage. I'm sure that's what's hung her up on Del. She needs to have some attention paid to her, some encouragement, some—well, maybe some affection."

As though embarrassed at having come so close to saying outright she wanted Naline seduced, she interrupted herself. "You didn't have any parallel problems on the men's side, did you?"

"Ah ... I guess not. All of us are quite a bit older than Naline. All sort of—ah—settled for life in their personal orientation. If young Bendle hadn't died, perhaps then things might have been different. But all we had was a couple of fights when we got sick of being shut in by the snow."

"A couple!" Ornelle snorted. "We had a couple a day— or that's what it felt like. But ... What do you think, Lex?"

He didn't answer for a moment. He was working a calculation in his head, not cynically, just assessing facts. There was a slight majority of women now; marginally hardier than men, they had lost seven to the males' fourteen and fewer of them were falling sick. On the other hand you had to consider the question of their breeding ability. . . .

His mind revolted. He wasn't trained to that peak of detachment, though he knew it was required of polymaths when they took up their ultimate posts. He couldn't think of the potential advantage of having the youngest girl in the group as his wife, because of her longer fertile future.

"Sorry," he said, and had to lick his lips. "I can't."

"Very well." She sighed. "I didn't know you already had a girl, but—"

"I don't. I don't even have my eye on one. But there's a point of principle. Our survival here may ultimately depend on honesty, facing the facts as they are. The repercussions of acting a lie, as you've suggested, could be disastrous. No matter how unselfish the underlying motive is. Good night, Ornelle."

All the way back to the single men's house he was trying to decide whether, true or not, he should have said that.

There were only about half a dozen men in the house, chatting among themselves; the rest were out, a few working, most relaxing.

He couldn't help wondering whether one of them was with Delvia.

◆ VII ◆

"What do you think, Lex?" Jerode said. He was visibly tense as the members of the general assembly gathered—everyone who had survived the winter, the poisons, the sickness, the cold—to take stock of their situation and hear what the steering committee recommended.

Standing in the shadow of the headquarters hut, watching the way people were grouping themselves as they sat on the gently rising ground and trying to read implications into their choice of near neighbors, Lex shook his head.

"I think Ornelle may have been only too right," he said.

"So do I." Jerode tapped a sheaf of documents in his hand. "We made out this list of priority jobs. I was wondering whether we ought not to have drawn up an assignment list, too, naming everyone."

"Why didn't you suggest it?"

"One: it's the kind of thing I've been relying on Arbogast to handle. It comes more readily to a ship's captain to think of duty rosters and suchlike. Two: it seems to me better to build around a nucleus of volunteers for every job, and either rely on them to invite capable assistance from the others, or shame the ones who hang back into finding work wherever they're needed."

"Sounds shrewd," Lex said.

"I did right, then?" Jerode sounded hungry for the answer.

"Doc, don't look to me," Lex said with some annoyance. "Everything's new here. We'll have to see if it works; if it doesn't, try something different. Now I wonder"—his voice dropped as his eyes roamed the growing crowd—"why Rothers is keeping those vacant spaces near the front. You know him, the man who used to be on the spaceport computing staff? Ah, of course. That must be it."

"What?" Jerode blinked at him.

44

"Manager Nanseltine and his wife aren't here yet. Nor is Delvia, come to that. The ones with rank hung over from home, and I much suspect the one who's going to acquire some here. By pecking order methods. Here they come."

Heads turned in the seated crowd. Arbogast was approaching, and with him, talking volubly, tall stout Nanseltine and his florid graying wife. The captain clearly was taking no notice, just enduring what was said.

"How did Nanseltine manage to retain so much flesh during the winter?" Jerode muttered.

"The rest of us lost some of it by sweating it off, not just by going hungry," Lex replied. "There's an exception."

"Yes, I guess so. . . . Well, here we go." Jerode sighed, and moved to welcome the captain.

The first fuss was over chairs for the Nanseltines. Two had been set on the verandah of the headquarters hut for Arbogast and Jerode—no one objected to these two being privileged—but everyone else was agreeable to using the ground. Then people behind the chairs which were brought for the Nanseltines complained their view was blocked, and a minor argument developed. Arbogast made no attempt to quiet it, simply sat staring at nothing.

That wasn't altogether without advantages, Lex thought. Leaning against the corner of the hut, careful not to dislodge any of its timbers, he studied the faces of the crowd. Yes, there were factions. On the useful side, those like Cheffy, Aldric, possibly Delvia: willing to face reality and work hard. Many of them were ringed around Bendle, with pens and scraps of "paper" ready to take notes. Others were grouped close to Fritch; these were members of his building team. Not for the first time Lex was grateful for the statistical accident which had produced a majority of people under forty and yet so few children. Of course, that had been due to the season. Nine out of every ten children in Zara's northern hemisphere had been on life-adaptation courses away from home at the time of the disaster.

Now Naline was the baby of them all, at sixteen. Bendle's son had been a few months younger, and there had been four infants. But they had all succumbed to a lung infection. . . .

Present, not past, he reminded himself sternly. On the useless side then—no, correction: the less useful side, because everyone here had to count—the Nanseltines and their cronies; you could spot them now, the ones complaining because they didn't have chairs too or because they didn't see why the Nanseltines should when they didn't. Also the fawners, like Rothers, of whom a cluster centered on Nanseltine's wife, saying of *course* MANAGER Nanseltine should have a chair.

And in the middle of these categories, almost half the total number: category undecided.

The arguments ended when Cheffy, with his characteristic tact, suggested moving the chairs to one side of the crowd where they would obstruct no one's view. With a sigh of relief Jerode turned to Arbogast. An expectant hush fell.

Slowly Arbogast drew himself to his feet. He looked dreadfully old, as though the past day had aged him fifty years. But his voice was firm, and carried across the crowd.

He said, "Fellow . . . castaways! Up till now you have in a sense been—well, under my command. I have not objected. In space, and directly following our arrival, I was fitted for it, I think. But all I know is space and spaceships. On a planet's surface, I think it better for everyone if I relinquish this unenviable position to someone suited to the new circumstances."

Lex looked at Nanseltine to see if he realized what was coming. Nanseltine didn't react, but his wife did.

The corners of Lex's mouth turned down sharply. *Might have guessed. . . .*

"I propose therefore," Arbogast went on, "that this assembly should be presided over by someone we all respect and admire for his invaluable work. Dr. Jerode, will you. . . ?"

He made a quick flourish; then he picked up his chair and carried it to the side of the crowd distant from Nanseltine. Finally catching on, the latter looked startled —and his wife, furious. A buzz of comment rose and faded.

Jerode looked at Lex and shrugged. He turned and called across the crowd, "Is that acceptable?"

There was a ripple of applause.

"Very well, then." The doctor shuffled his notes. "As you know, our position has much improved in spite of . . ."

When Jerode got around to describing the urgent work ahead, Lex was able to sort a great many more of the crowd into their respective categories. The useful ones frowned, but were cheered by realizing what a well-planned program had been devised. The less-than-useful also frowned, then gave up listening and began to mutter restively among themselves. Still, there was no real trouble until Fritch finished talking about work on the accomodation. Nobody was minded to object to improving their living conditions.

But then Bendle talked about possible new food supplies, and went on at great length and with a lot of jargon, and people fretted visibly. Jerode's voice shook when he rose to call on Aldric next, to discuss water supplies, the manufacture of tools, and other technical matters.

"The ship!" someone cried at the back of the crowd. "Hey, what about the ship?"

"Yes! Yes!" Twenty voices shouted agreement, and a pattern of nods made heads wave like grass under wind. Jerode, uncertain, stood blinking, and Aldric—on his feet to approach the verandah—hesitated with his notes in his hand.

"Very well," the doctor said at last. "If it's your wish I'll call on Lex, who visited the ship yesterday."

The useless ones were the ones who applauded now. The others only came alert. Lex unfolded his long legs and made the one step up to take station beside Jerode.

"The ship," he said in a clear, penetrating voice, "is about one-third under mud, about one-third under water. Salt water. A highly corrosive liquid. I entered it through an open cargo lock"—his eyes flicked to Arbogast, who winced, but he had to rub in the facts—"and found that when it rolled over, everything unsecured was smashed. What was not broken by being flung against the wall or ceiling is in unsalvageable condition. At least two explosions occurred in the fuel-reserve room and shattered most of the drive gear. Sand and mud—hundreds of tons of it—have sifted inside. Sea-creatures and weed have taken possession. This is exactly what we were expecting."

He paused, assessing the impact of what he was saying.

"Accordingly," he resumed, "the best we can make of the ship from now on is a stockpile of metal and other raw materials. And it isn't going to be easy to get at it, either. We'll have to develop some way of powering cutting-tools under water, means of floating large pieces back to shore—rafts, maybe—and solve other problems which will take so much time I can't recommend them for immediate attention. All I can recommend right now is stripping out loose fragments that can be brought back in the boat."

He glanced at Jerode. "I think that's all I can say."

"Thank you, Lex. As you said, I think we expected the substance of your report. Now we'll hear Aldric, and—"

"Just a moment!" That was Rothers, sitting beside the Nanseltines, having moved when they shifted their chairs. Lex glanced his way. Nanseltine's wife was speaking urgently to her husband and several people nearby were nodding vigorously. Now, ponderous, Nanseltine got up.

"Who went over the ship?" he demanded, setting his shoulders back. "No one but you?"

"That's correct," Lex said, climbing back on the verandah.

"No one but you!" Old mannerisms were returning to Nanseltine, that was obvious. "Are we to take it, then, that this—this defeatist view is based exclusively on your inexpert observations?"

"You're welcome to put on a suit and come down with me to see for yourself. I think we might find one to fit you." Lex weighted the words with deliberate sarcasm.

"Don't descend to personal insult, young man!" Nanseltine glowered, while those of the crowd who hadn't got Lex's point at once got it now and smiled regardless of which side they were on. Meantime, the former continental manager continued, "What I, and a lot of other people here, want to know, is why we don't have the expert opinion of a spaceman instead of this—this amateur evaluation."

There was silence. Someone whispered, "Which spaceman?" The words carried, and Arbogast heard. With dignity, head erect, the old man—suddenly it was natural to think of him by that term—rose and faced Nanseltine.

"Manager Nanseltine!" he said. "Perhaps you're not aware of the condition of the *spacemen* among us! You seem aware of rather little of what's going on here!"

A ragged cheer commented on the rebuke.

"I had four men in my crew! One had his skull cracked by a bale of goods that fell on him while we were clearing our holds to make room for you people! One is present, who had to have a leg amputated after frostbite. One was trying to inspect the ropewalk across the river in a gale, lost his grip, and fell into the water. No doubt he was swept out to sea and drowned. And one was on ground leave on Zara. That leaves myself, and Lex, who volunteered to work under me during our flight and in whom I, if not you, repose some confidence as a result.

"I cannot deny, however, that I had intended to go down and inspect my ship. I didn't do so, for reasons I—" His voice cracked, and he ended on a lower tone—"I would rather not try to explain. I will only apologize. Excuse me."

He lowered his head and walked away, out of sight as he turned the corner of the nearest building.

Nanseltine had the wit to realize that if he pushed his line of questioning any further now, he would turn his audience against him. Making the most of a bad job, he said loudly, "Since the captain is prepared to trust Lex's judgment, that will suffice." And he sat down and shut up.

Unfortunately not everyone else had that much grace. Rothers, the former computer chief, jumped up in his turn.

"You mean we're not even going to try to refit the ship and get off this—this pestilential mudball?"

You could see the words hitting and hurting the useless ones.

"It's a heap of scrap—weren't you listening?" called Cheffy.

"Oh, be quiet!" chorused a dozen young voices. For a moment it looked as though the trouble were going to die down. But then—and Lex clenched his fists in impotent anger—Ornelle tossed fuel on the flames.

"The party up on the plateau had a ship too," she said. "That one can't be under water. And we haven't heard anything from them, so it's likely they have no further use for it. Why aren't you mounting an expedition to go and see?"

That lunatic proposition snatched at the fancy of those who would rather delude than save themselves. At once a roar of excitement went up. People leaped to their feet —Nanseltine again, Rothers again, forty or fifty in all— demanding to be heard. In vain Jerode shouted for order.

Lex bit his lip and looked toward Ornelle. Her face was very white and she met his gaze defiantly.

He drew a deep breath and let out a sudden wordless bellow, so startling that everyone froze in surprise. Before they could recover he had lanced a question at Rothers.

"The ship repair yard at your port—did it handle ships that size?"

"Why—why, of course!" the man answered.

"How big was it?"

"Ah . . ." He licked his lips. "About a mile and a half square, I guess."

"How much of the operation was done by hand?"

"Why—why, none, of course!"

There was a laugh. It came from, of all people, Delvia. Obviously she had her wits about her.

"Doc, a motion," Lex said quickly. "I think this calls for a vote of confidence in the steering committee."

"Just what I was thinking," Jerode said with relief. "Those who—"

But he didn't have to take a count. It was passed by acclamation, a majority of over two-thirds. Lex noticed, with interest, that it was Delvia who triggered off the clapping.

Frustrated for the moment, the useless ones made no more trouble. But Lex was profoundly glad that the question of Delvia's pregnancy hadn't come up after all; Jerode simply didn't mention it, and was wise not to in the heated atmosphere of this meeting.

So they'd got away with it this time, at least.

It wasn't until the assembly ended just before dusk that Arbogast's body was found among the rocks fringing the beach, with a spent energy gun clasped in the right hand which was now his only recognizable feature. He had opened the beam to widest spread and turned the weapon against himself.

◆ VIII ◆

The shadow of Arbogast's suicide lay chill across the hot bright days that followed. Towing a sled laden with scrap salvaged from the ship up the beach to where Aldric and his gang were working on the solar boilers and stills,

Lex wondered how long their precarious balance was going to last. Twenty days had elapsed, then thirty, without disaster. But he had a fearful feeling that time was gnawing at their psychological props like termites, and eventually . . .

Aldric raised a face half masked with dark glasses to acknowledge the delivery. Lex tipped the scrap to the ground with a clatter and stood back, wiping sweat from his forehead.

"How are things with you, Aldric?" he said, low-voiced. "Going smoothly, by the look of all this."

Aldric hesitated. Then, pretending to examine the scrap piece by piece, he moved close enough to Lex to whisper.

"No, Lex—not so smooth. Matter of fact, I'd been wanting a word with you, and now might be as good a time as any. Here, let's stroll along the beach a bit."

"Sure." Lex caught the handle of his sled in one hand and drew it behind as he fell in alongside. "These sleds are OK on the beach," he muttered, "but we'll need wheeled trucks some time soon. . . . Sorry. What were you going to say?"

"Among other things, I'm wondering how hot it's going to be in midsummer." Aldric paused, judging they were out of earshot of his crew. "I'm getting a lot of complaints about noontide work, and not frivolous ones, either. I had a case of heatstroke yesterday. Cheffy says some hot-climate countries back on Earth used to have a period for sleep in the middle of the day. I'm not so sure that would be the answer; it's easier to stretch to a day longer than Earth-basic, harder to cut down to a shorter one. And that would mean, in effect, having two short days. Halves of days."

"If Cheffy says people adjusted to it, he's probably right," Lex said. "Whether we'd be willing to is another matter. But surely if the heat does become unbearable . . . Well, what else could you do with the time you can't work, except doze?"

"I know what you mean," Aldric grunted. "On or off the job!"

Shading his eyes, Lex looked along the beach. In the near foreground was Aldric's domain: in a weird spidery layout there were solar boilers that doubled as distillation equipment interspersed with crude turbine generators. The drive of the ship had been cannibalized for many of the parts, once everybody was convinced there was no but absolutely *no* hope of repairing it. Ornelle had held out for nearly a week.

Beyond, fishing nets hung in the sun on racks, drying while girls checked the knots. Bendle had succeeded in preparing an antidote for the commonest allergens in the sea-life, and although they looked revolting even after they'd been cooked half a dozen species were now providing welcome and quite tasty variety in their diet. Back inland, ground was being cleared for planting—Bendle was up there with his team right now, studying the reproductive processes of their first standby, the salad-tree, in the hope of selecting for the strain with the best leaf-yield.

In the other direction the solar collector sheets were all spread out. Accumulators were being charged continuously. He saw Delvia, burned brown now, laughing and joking with a gang of Fritch's men who were waiting for replacement accumulators for their power-tools.

Inland again there was a noise of sawing punctuated by crashes. Timber being felled. He could just discern a line of yellow trunks drying in the sun. The odd-shaped whitish forms of fishingbirds rested on them like wilting flowers. Their gummy black droppings were all over the beach—not to mention the roofs and, worse still, the pathways of the town. They were becoming a distinct nuisance, and some means would have to be found to frighten them away.

"I wonder where those birds go for the winter," Lex murmured. "Maybe we should follow their example."

Aldric gave a harsh laugh. "Won't do us much good," he said. "One of Bendle's people told me about them. They aren't migratory. They encapsulate—secrete a kind of gelatinous shell for themselves—and spend the winter stuck to the rocks. They thought they were eggs at first, but the eggs are being laid now."

Lex nodded absently; the list of curious habits among the local fauna was too long already for him to be surprised. Besides, he had been carefully educated to expect the unexpected. He said, "Well, if heat's our only problem, we can either develop the siesta habit as Cheffy suggests—which won't be as hard as you make out, if you remember that the midsummer days are very long—or else plan a secondary program of jobs for everyone that they can fill in with in the shade for an hour or two either side of noon."

"I don't think a change of work is the answer," Aldric said. "It's a question of—well, frayed tempers. Look. I gave Rothers a job to keep him sweet, melting down scrap in a solar furnace, with half a dozen assistants under him. I thought a bit of petty authority would satisfy him."

"It didn't?"

"It did not. He had an argument with one of his helpers, lost his temper, hit the guy—knocked him against the back of the furnace-mirror and bent it clear out of shape. That's why it isn't out here working. I had to detail my two best handymen to restore the curvature. Meantime Rothers is snarling at everyone and slowing down my work."

He made a gesture that embraced the entire field of view. "All this looks great. Signs of progress. But underneath it's ready to explode."

"You don't have to tell me." Lex sighed. "And I go right along with your point that a change of work won't be enough. It's about time we cheered ourselves up somehow—sort of congratulated ourselves on our marvelous achievements. I'll talk to Jerode about it, make a report to the next assembly. Initiate some hobbies, perhaps, stimulate competition, provide a few luxuries. . . . I've been wondering about music. We could handcraft some instruments, I guess."

"Just so long as somebody's thinking about the problem," Aldric said. "I have too much to do to waste time worrying. Just thought I'd tell you."

Yes, Lex thought, the physical problems could be overcome. Given the rest of the summer, the town could be made moderately comfortable, twice as warm as last winter, with far more room for people to spread out. The food problem was almost licked. There was adequate water. Clothing was still a difficulty, but it was amazing how long fraying fabrics could be made to hold together. Besides, in this heat everyone preferred to wear the minimum.

A point struck him. He glanced toward Delvia again. Yes, Naline was there. While Fritch's men were loading up with charged accumulators, she was keeping her back turned so she wouldn't have to watch Delvia laughing and chatting.

It hadn't come to an explosion yet—but it would. Damn Delvia! Her old tabard was becoming a collection of rags linked by threads; instead of darning it like the other girls she had reduced it to a kind of kilt, thereby proving that she possessed the handsomest bust among the refugees.

And yet she was a tough and reliable worker herself. How could one reprimand one of the most useful people around? She hadn't been assigned to her particular job. She had just seen that someone would have to make sure charged accumulators were in regular supply, so she had proceeded to coordinate the arrangements in an orderly and economical manner. And Naline, of course, had shadowed her.

Would it serve any purpose to bring her onto the steering committee? Jerode kept asking him that question; every time Lex returned the same answer. She and Ornelle would waste hours wrangling over personal differences, and Ornelle was coping usefully enough with the human problems she had been allotted. The register of intended pregnancies, for instance—that had been her idea. It would be open for another month at most. No winter births if humanly possible.

But Delvia . . . In the end there had been no fuss over terminating her pregnancy. When she was told about it following the stock-taking assembly, she had meekly accepted Jerode's rebuke and demanded a shot to get rid of it.

The idea wasn't one to which he could bring many of the refugees around, but Lex was beginning to suspect that this involuntary colony could do with many more Delvias and far fewer Ornelles and Nalines.

Dragging his sled, he made his way back toward the point where his gang of amateur salvagemen were checking equipment after the morning's diving. Spacesuits, tough as they were, might tear on a sharp projection; hatchets—essential now that the summer life of the sea was teeming—were blunted and had to be reground; one helmet was cracked and would have to be patched somehow; the boat was lying bottom-up on the sand while one of the girls, her pink tonguetip between her teeth, was chipping away masses of hard-shelled sessile animals which had clung to the hull.

He was lucky, Lex thought. He had a keen team. The strong element of physical danger in this underwater work had sorted them out for him.

Not to mention their willingness to work under a young leader. . . .

"Lex! Lex!"

He spun around. Running toward him from the direction of the river was Cheffy, waving and shouting. One glance told him this was urgent. He left the sled where it was and ran to meet him.

"What is it?" he called, thinking over a whole range of possible catastrophes. Cheffy was working on what they referred to, with a wry awareness of exaggeration, as the civil engineering projects of the town: water supply, sanitation, and heating for the inevitable winter.

"Just you come and look!" Cheffy snapped, whirling around and making back the way he had come. Better built for running than he had been when he landed here, he still was going too fast to have breath to spare for talk.

It was only a matter of moments before they came in sight of what had been yesterday a wide calm expanse of steadily flowing water, discolored by suspended silt and the larvae of some as-yet unidentified species of aquatic creature that metamorphosed to the adult stage when the river carried it into salt water.

Yesterday? This morning, even, when Lex came down to start work!

Now it was reduced to a trickle. Irregular curves of mud had been exposed; a few writhing creatures lay gasping in puddles, and water-weeds were already turning gray-yellow and deliquescing into a stinking mess from exposure to the full sun. The mouth of the estuary normally passed such a flow that the course of the fresh water could be traced a hundred feet from shore. Now the sea was trespassing into the riverbed.

Lex halted, appalled. They had staked everything on the river! Cheffy was planning to draw water for drinking and washing via a sedimentation system a mile upstream, to replace the crude bucket-hoists they still depended on. They had decided to install piped water for every house and flush-sanitation for every twenty-five people. At the moment, since the sea was barred to them for swimming anyway and there was no tide to return the effluent, they were content to let the offshore current disperse their

sewage, which was at least an advance on the crude
latrines of the first month here; but pipes made of hollow
tree-trunks sealed with plastic film were being readied—
one and a half miles of them—to take their drains well
away from the town.

And now . . . this!

He wasn't the only person Cheffy had summoned to
witness the horrifying phenomenon. Jerode was here already. Work had stopped on all the riverside projects, and
members of the subteams in charge of them were clustered
around, speculating in low, worried voices. On glancing
upstream Lex saw that two or three of the team who had
been constructing the sedimentation tanks were making
their way down the middle of the drying riverbed.

Jerode, acknowledging his arrival with a nod, called
to Lex. "What do you make of all this?"

"When did it happen?" Lex countered grimly.

"The level began to drop about an hour ago, maybe
an hour and a half," Cheffy said. "It was slow to start with,
so I guess we didn't notice for a while. Then it dropped
really sharply. You could watch it going down, like water
running out of a tub. Do you think it's a seasonal stoppage? Because if so we can just tear up our plans."

"No, not a seasonal stoppage," Lex said. "Remember
we got here at the end of the summer, and this river was
still deep and wide. Besides, if it were only a question
of the headwaters not being fed—with snow or whatever
—the stream would dry up slowly over days or weeks.
This is due to a blockage higher up. A solid obstacle."

Jerode, who had come closer, nodded. "That makes
sense. What could have caused it—a landslide? Or . . ."
He scratched his bald pate thoughtfully. "I seem to recall
that back on Earth they have an animal which dams
rivers. A—a beeger?"

"Beaver!" Cheffy exclaimed. "Yes, of course. Lex, do
you reckon there could be a dam-building animal here?"

"There not only could be," Lex said after a pause.
"There is."

Cheffy and Jerode stared at him, puzzled.

"Man," Lex said. "If you remember, we found that
this river leads directly to where the other party set
down."

"Lex, that's absurd!" Jerode snapped. "We've tried and
tried to make contact with them—we're still trying now
and then—and there's total radio silence. They must be

dead!" And added in a lower tone, "Much as it galls me to find I'm agreeing with Ornelle."

Lex shrugged. "Didn't mean you to take me so seriously, Doc. All I was saying was: it's possible for all we know."

"Look—whatever it is that stopped the water," Cheffy said, "we've simply got to get it back! With explosives if we have to."

Jerode hesitated. "Yes, of course. . . . Well, I was intending to put a proposal to the next assembly, since things are—I mean were—going so well. Another expedition to the plateau, to find out if there are any survivors up there, see if their ship's worth cannibalizing if there aren't. As a matter of fact"—he rounded on Lex—"I was going to ask if you'd lead it."

◈ IX ◈

The news about the river spread like wildfire. Within half an hour all work had stopped except Fritch's, and he was keeping his gang on the job only because they were halfway through raising a main roof-beam, thirty feet long, thick, and very heavy. Everyone who had been on the beach drifted back, even Lex's salvage team, and the rest of Cheffy's upstream workers came shouting to know what they should do now. It was inevitable that someone should suggest an emergency assembly.

As usual, rumors that an assembly was in the offing brought the self-important—Nanseltine, Rothers, and their kind—clustering around Jerode like flies on honey, to pester him with ill-considered ideas and nonnegotiable demands. It took the better part of an hour to drive people back to work with assurances that the assembly would meet at dusk.

Then Jerode sent for the members of the steering committee and called them to the headquarters hut to discuss their only reasonable course of action.

"I don't see why we have to argue," Fritch said. He seemed more annoyed by being called away from work than worried by the loss of the river. "Someone's got to walk upstream and find the blockage, then either clear it or, if it's too big, come back for help. All we have to decide is who shall go."

Jerode cleared his throat. "I had it in mind to propose Lex."

Everyone except Ornelle nodded approval. Jerode added, "Though he hasn't said he's willing yet."

"Oh, I'll go," Lex said with a shrug. "And you won't lose much work from my team, either. We've got about as much as we can out of our own ship now. Anything more will require flame-cutters, and until we can stabilize an underwater arc or maybe find a way of making pure fluorine we have nothing to touch the metal of the hull. Oxyhydrogen flames are easy, but they're not hot enough. So I think it would be a good idea if, after we clear the blockage, I take my team on up to the plateau. If Ornelle's belief is justified, our experience in carving up our own ship will be very useful when it comes to tackling the other one."

"I thought you'd come around to thinking the others might be alive after all," Cheffy said. "Might have built a dam."

"I only meant to point out," Lex said patiently, "that a dam-building animal does exist here. I'm sorry if I answered your question too literally."

"Yes, Bendle?" Jerode said hastily. Cheffy sounded uncharacteristically bad-tempered. Well he might be, with all his cherished schemes hanging fire for an indefinite period.

The gray-haired biologist leaned forward, rubbing a strawberry rash on his cheek, souvenir of an encounter with the plant they had nicknamed blisterweed. "I'm not sure about Lex taking his entire salvage team. I suggest you take one of my people, someone intimately acquainted with the local flora and fauna. Perhaps one of Fritch's people, too, in case you need expert advice on how best to demolish the blockage."

"Sounds sensible," Fritch said reluctantly. "Though I hope you don't keep my man away too long, Lex."

"I'll try not to," Lex murmured. He could read their opinions on their faces: *He's a capable young fellow, tough, levelheaded—and rather him than me.*

"Very well, then," Jerode said. "Now the question of numbers. How many can we spare altogether?"

Everyone looked at Lex. "How many do you think you need?" Aldric demanded.

"Half a dozen should be enough," Lex answered. "We only have seven energy guns."

"Are you thinking of taking them all?" Ornelle burst out. "Suppose while you're away we—"

"Suppose nothing!" Fritch snapped. "He's right. They're more important to people venturing into strange country than they are to us down here."

"But if we lose—"

"You'd rather lose people than guns?"

Ornelle subsided, cheeks fiery. Fritch went on, "And what rations should we give you, Lex—enough for a week?"

"About that. We could carry more, but I don't think we could carry water for much longer. It's heavy, and in this heat we're likely to drink a lot. Could you ask for a volunteer from your gang, then? And you, Bendle? I know who else from my own team I'd like to have with me."

"That seems to be settled, then," Fritch said with satisfaction. "Doc, while I happen to be here: about that hut you want expanded into a proper infirmary . . ."

The assembly met in gathering darkness. The lights taken from the ship, which had been used throughout last winter, had begun to fail, and there was so far no way of fabricating replacements, though the informative Cheffy had referred to lamp filaments made of carbonized thread. Accordingly posts had been set up on which resinous torches flared and reeked. Curiously, people seemed to like this crude illumination, as though fire symbolized some innate friendliness in nature.

There had been no trouble picking Lex's team. From among his own salvage workers he invited Minty, a wiry woman in her early thirties with the spare figure of an athlete, and brawny, imperturbable Aykin; these two had been among the first couples to indicate their intention of starting a family, and Lex took that as a sign of determination.

Then, before he spoke to the other pair he'd had in mind, a point struck him which he'd overlooked in committee. He himself knew the route to the other party's site because he had accompanied Arbogast when he led a brief and hazardous trip there. Of course, by then the country had been dying toward winter; at this time of

year it would look very different. Nonetheless, just in case
something happened to himself, it would be a good idea
to have one person along who had also been that way
before. He knew who he wanted, too: a tall fair man
called Baffin, who had studied hydraulics and hydro-
dynamics and ought in any case to get another look at the
river.

"Oh, take him!" Cheffy said. "There's nothing for him
to do until the water comes back!"

Fritch recommended a sober young man called
Aggereth, to whom Lex bunked close in the single men's
house. He thought the choice a good one; Aggereth was
reliable and hard-working. Bendle's recommendation was
a woman, Lodette, plump-faced and dark-skinned. She
had been concentrating on the study of the inland fauna
and knew almost as much about it as Bendle himself.

Lastly, Jerode came hurrying in search of him with a
new suggestion: should the party not include one of the
girls who had constituted themselves an emergency nursing
staff last winter and were now spending most of their
time studying medicine and surgery from the ship's manu-
als? Zanice would be pleased to go along, a gray-eyed
blonde woman of forty-odd, known to Lex by sight like
everyone in the town, though he could not remember ever
exchanging a word with her.

So: a balanced group, with a good range of skills. Lex
was well-pleased with the outcome.

Against the risk that not everyone else would be,
though, and in accordance with Jerode's principle of
allowing people to be seen to volunteer when a tough job
was ahead, even if in fact they'd made up their minds long
before, Lex asked his chosen six to scatter themselves
among the crowd at assembly time and come forward
when he called for them. There was no risk of a rush of
volunteers; there would be a psychological lag. What he
was worried about was the problem of people who might
try to argue that he was unsuited to lead the party. In
the event, no one actually rose and said so out loud.

Nor, fortunately, did anybody—even Ornelle—harp on
the expedition's subsidiary purpose, that of visiting the
other party's site. It was quietly accepted as a logical
thing to do while people were upriver.

The questions were much what he had expected. Was
the river dry simply because it was summer? There hadn't
been any rain here for nearly two months, after all, had

there? What about arrangements for drinking and washing until the river was flowing again? Why had the self-appointed leaders of the community allowed such a thing to happen? (The last wasn't said in so many words, but it was implicit in the acid face of Nanseltine's wife, who spent most of the meeting having a furious but whispered argument with her husband. However, Nanseltine seemed to be learning a bit of sense at long last and didn't rise to her gibes.)

Lex was pleased when a ripple of laughter effectively silenced Rothers, who had raised some totally irrelevant point, and left Jerode free to call on him as nominated leader of the expedition.

On his request for companions, the six got up—not too hurriedly—and stood while he noted them, nodded, and beckoned them to him. But there was one other volunteer, not someone he had expected, indeed almost the last person he would have imagined as willing to go . . . let alone eager.

"I want to come," Delvia said in a clear firm voice.

Now what was to be done? Lex's mind raced. He saw that Naline—still, despite everything, dogging the older girl's footsteps—was reaching up and tugging at Delvia's hand to make her sit down again. Impatiently Delvia shook the fingers loose. Lex began to recite the qualifications of those he wanted as companions, hoping to show that every important requirement was taken care of, but no one paid any attention. They were looking at Delvia.

Although it was cool after sunset, she had added nothing to her working dress—undress, rather. Now she was apparently regretting it, with several hundred pairs of eyes on her. Perhaps embarrassment would change her mind, make her sit down? No, Lex decided regretfully. Not in Delvia's case.

Well, he'd have to improvise a reason for turning her down.

"Uh . . . the team needn't be any larger anyway, and besides we're already going to deprive the town of several key people while we're away. One more still would be—"

"Starshine," Delvia interrupted. "I'm not 'key people.' What I do is so simple I mainly figured it out by myself. And Naline has worked with me right from the start. There's nothing I can do that she can't."

Transparently true. Lex gave Jerode a worried glance,

wondering if the doctor had an inspiration. Taking his momentary silence for resignation, however, Delvia started to pick her way through the seated crowd.

"No!" Suddenly there was a shrill cry, and Naline was on her feet, clawing at Delvia's back. "No! You aren't going to *go!*"

Her hand caught the piece of cloth which was Delvia's only covering; there was a ripping sound and it tore free. With an oath Delvia spun around.

Tears coursing down her cheeks, voice rough-edged with hysteria, Naline shrieked, "Why don't you say why you want to go? Why don't you say it's to get away from me? Why don't you say it's so you can screw Lex the way you've had every other man you could drag into the bushes?" She raised the cloth in her hand, head-high, and waved it wildly. "What do you want with this, anyway? Practically everyone else has had your clothes off already!"

She hurled the rag away from her, whirled, and with her hands out before her like a blind girl fled into the darkness.

There was total stillness, as though the audience were trying to believe that this thing hadn't happened. It was broken by Delvia in a tone of absolute self-possession.

She said, "May I have my tabard back, please?"

It was passed to her. She sorted it out after a fashion and knotted it about her hips more or less as it had been before. Then, with arrogance that took Lex's breath away, she resumed walking toward him.

"Someone had better go after Naline," Lex said to Jerode out of the side of his mouth.

"Yes, of course," the doctor muttered. He looked around for someone suitable, but Zanice had caught the exchange and was already on her way. Lex drew a deep breath. Well, it was being forced on him.

"Delvia!" he said. "Please go back to your place."

She stopped, cocking her head. "Oh! So you're afraid Naline was telling the truth, are you?"

"I don't think she said anything that was news to us," Lex said brutally. "Whether you can be blamed for it or not, Delvia, everyone knows you're impulsive. We're going into wild country, facing unknown dangers. You'd be too much of a risk."

"I see," Delvia said after a pause. "Very well, you know best."

With perfectly good grace—or so it appeared—she went

back to where she had been sitting. A buzz of comment rose and at Jerode's bidding stilled again. After that the meeting proceeded smoothly to its end.

But for some reason Delvia kept smiling, and it disturbed Lex considerably that he couldn't figure out why.

◈ **X** ◈

"Keeping radio watch!" Elbing said ruefully. "Well, it's about all I'm fit for now, I guess." He lifted his peg-leg from the ground to relieve the pressure on his stump. He was the last surviving member of Arbogast's crew; like many spacemen, he suffered from circulatory disorders, and the frost of last winter had cost him his right leg below the knee.

Lex clapped him on the shoulder. "It'll be good to have someone listening out that we know is accustomed to the job. Come on in the hut. Aykin is figuring out a backpack for our set."

Gesturing for Elbing to precede him, he glanced around. The air was muggy and oppressive, and dark clouds fringed the seaward horizon. There was tension in the air. It tantalized his mind. He felt as though there were some necessary provision he ought to have made for the town, yet he could not determine what.

He shrugged. Necessary, in any case, didn't mean possible. He followed Elbing into the hut.

Their only radios were from the starship, of course: big and heavy, not intended to be carried from place to place nor to be run from portable accumulators. Aykin had devised a rough wooden case attached to a shoulder-harness; just as Lex and Elbing entered, he was slipping out of it, easing it gently onto a table.

"How are you getting on?" Lex demanded. "How many extra accumulators will we have to carry?"

"None," Aykin said with satisfaction. "Look. This is an idea Minty hit on." He picked up a short length of metal tube with wire wrapped around it. "The answer is to increase the length of the antenna. Minty suggested throwing this up over a tree-branch. I've just been trying it out, and it looks as though we'll be able to transmit and receive quite clearly on the low-power setting. So we won't need the extra accumulator."

"Ingenious." Elbing nodded, lowering himself stiffly to a chair. Lex frowned, not because the idea wasn't a good one, but because he felt he ought now to grasp the point he had been fumbling after.

He said slowly, "Did you follow up my suggestion—take one of the solar collector sheets, spread that out, and use it to drive the radio?" There was one drawback to that: it would mean transmitting during the day, when solar interference was at its worst, instead of at leisure when they made camp after nightfall, and in any case the problem had been solved. But association of ideas might lead him to the one that was eluding him.

In the far corner Minty and Lodette both looked up. They had been poring over a list on a shelf nailed to the wall.

"Lodette says if we follow the river we may hardly see the sun at all," Minty declared.

"That's right." The plump-faced biologist nodded. "I don't know if you've been far inland this summer, but the vegetation upstream is *thick*."

"Besides"—Aykin laid the wire antenna back on the table—"it's clouding over. It may even be going to storm."

Lex snapped his fingers. That was it: going to storm—wires in trees—lightning conductors! He said, "Back in a moment." And hurried off to find Jerode.

The hut which Fritch was intending to turn into a proper infirmary by adding a new wing stood a little apart from the other buildings. It was the logical place to look for the doctor. Casting anxious glances at the clouds on the horizon and wondering whether the expedition might have to be postponed, Lex strode toward the curtained doorway. When he was a few paces away the curtain swung back and Ornelle emerged, her face pale.

On seeing Lex she froze for a moment, then let the curtain fall and continued forward.

"Is Jerode in there?" Lex demanded.

"Yes, but you can't see him. He's busy." There was a bitter ring to Ornelle's voice which dismayed him.

"Why? Is something wrong?"

"Yes. Something you could have prevented. Only you said it was a question of principle not to. Naline has tried to follow Arbogast's example. Jerode says she'll live, but it looks as though she's blinded herself. Are you pleased at what you've done?"

"Why? Over Delvia?" Lex demanded, forcing himself to disregard the gibe.

"What do you think?"

"Exactly how did it happen?"

"She and Delvia were charging the energy guns for your expedition," Ornelle said bitingly. "I imagine they had an argument. Maybe Delvia said straight out that she'd used Naline as a toy to pass the winter and that was all their relationship meant to her. Anyway, Naline took one of the guns and went off among the trees. Bendle found her when he heard her moaning. The gun wasn't charged—it only flashed. But that was enough to put out her eyes."

"And Delvia?"

"Her!" Ornelle stamped her foot. "Still charging your guns, I guess. Sooner or later she'll notice that one is missing. Maybe she noticed already. But I haven't seen her come looking for it."

Lex drew a deep breath. He said, "You're determined to lay the blame for this on me, aren't you?"

Ornelle looked at him with smoldering eyes.

"*My* expedition, *my* guns, *my* responsibility!" Lex rapped. "Now you listen to me, Ornelle! I'm tired of this and I'm not going to put up with any more. Have you done anything to help Naline? Well, have you? Have you even tackled Delvia about it?"

Ornelle flinched. Defensively she countered, "I asked you to—"

"Why me? You watched this from the beginning and you didn't interfere—neither you nor any other of the supposedly responsible women in the house. All winter you let it stew; then the most you were willing to do was try to dump the chore of picking up the pieces on my shoulders. I am *not* going to carry your guilt for you; nor is anyone else. Do you understand?"

Ornelle's mouth worked. Suddenly her mask broke. She screamed a filthy name at him and slapped him on the cheek. He rode the blow impassively.

"Bastard!" she shrieked. "All you men are bastards!

You won't hear a word against that bitch, that whore, that—!"

He moved now, caught her arms and twisted them dexterously behind her, locking his steel-strong fingers around both her wrists. The curtain of the hut parted to reveal a startled Jerode.

Lex shut off Ornelle's obscene mouthings with the palm of his free hand. He said, "Tranquilizer shot, Doc. She's in a bad state—hysterical jealousy. Shall I carry her inside?"

"Uh—if you can!" said the astonished doctor.

Lex could. A few moments later Ornelle lay in drugged slumber on one of the medical examination couches.

"What the hell happened?" Jerode demanded.

Lex explained. "I ought to have realized it before," he finished. "She's crazy-jealous of Delvia, who doesn't let our predicament stop her getting what fun she can out of life. I was thrown off track by her saying she was concerned about Naline because she had two daughters back on Zara." He noticed in passing that he had given up saying "back home." So had virtually everybody else but a handful of what he regarded as the useless ones.

"You think—" Jerode began. Lex cut him short.

"I think you'd better find out what really happened in the single women's house during the winter. In detail. Next year we might prevent a repetition. Ornelle faked her disinterest. I'd guess that she wanted to mother Naline, to provide a surrogate for her lost daughters, and Naline wouldn't play, and took refuge with the least motherly of the other women. I'm afraid we may well have more nervous collapses of this type among women who have lost families and feel obscurely guilty, like Ornelle, about doing anything to replace them."

"It fits," Jerode said heavily. "And I ought to have figured it out myself, even though I'm a physical doctor and not a psychologist. I guess pressure of administration has taken my mind off my real job. And . . . Lex, I have to say this. You're partly to blame for that, aren't you?"

There was a long pause. During it, Lex reviewed everything that had happened to him so far on this planet. The bitter disappointment of not continuing to fulfill his great ambition still lingered; it would linger, perhaps, all his life. And yet he was no longer faced with the daunting prospect of decades of study, training, analyzing, examination, guesstimating. . . .

Here, after all, was a world. Brand-new. More likely to be ultimately habitable than not. And wasn't that the root of his ambition—to have a new world?

Eventually he turned away. His back to Jerode, he said, "I know. I'm sorry. Ornelle tried to load me with a responsibility which wasn't mine, and I lost my temper because I'm ashamed of not accepting a responsibility which really does belong to me. We can't go on burdening you with all the administrative work. When we come back from this trip, I'll turn the salvage team over to Minty and Aykin and get on with my proper job."

Jerode exhaled like a man coming up from an unendurable time under water. He said, "Lex, I can't tell you how glad I am. How soon are you going to be back?"

Smiling, composed again, Lex turned around. "Oh, about seven days altogether. That's assuming we can break through the blockage in the river. If the vegetation on the way is as thick as Lodette predicts—although I imagine we can get to the other party's site in about two days following the riverbed—we'll spend much longer coming back because we'll have to hack our way through dense undergrowth."

"Well, hurry!" Jerode said. His eyes were bright. Suddenly he laughed, and from the screened-off corner of the hut where Naline lay came an angry exclamation in Zanice's voice, asking him to be a little quieter.

When he had left Jerode, Lex was in a thoughtful mood. He had mentioned the lightning conductors, and Jerode had promised to refer the idea to Fritch. One tall metal post on high ground clear of the town should suffice.

The breakdown of Ornelle, though, had given him new cause to worry. How much of it was due to her belief, throughout the winter, that the other party was going to join forces this year and make life easier for everyone? How many other people, not so close to the edge of sanity, might yield to despair when objective news was brought back about the death of the other human group? Despite his comment to Jerode and Cheffy about there being a dam-building animal here, he no longer seriously considered it possible that there were survivors on the plateau.

He was not looking forward to what he expected to find up there.

Without realizing, he had let his feet carry him toward

the spot on the beach which Delvia had chosen as a site for her self-allotted task. Raising his eyes, he saw her ahead of him, surrounded by accumulators and solar collector sheets. On a rack of sticks tied with string were the seven energy guns the community possessed, fully charged.

So someone had brought back the gun Naline had used, and told her the story. Yet she was going on with her work, humming to herself. She had wrapped her tabard casually around her hips as before.

One of the accumulators was ready. She disconnected it, set it on another and those on another, and carried the three of them ten paces to a waiting handtruck. The ease with which she did it took Lex aback. The things were heavy; they doubled the depth of the prints her bare feet left in the sand.

He said, "Delvia!"

She straightened and turned, wiping sweating palms on her ragged kilt.

"They told you about Naline?" he said in a rough voice.

"Yes. One of Bendle's team brought the gun back." She waved at the rack. "They're all ready for you, by the way."

Lex simply stood, gazing at her. After a moment she snapped, "Well? Well? Are you waiting for me to burst into tears?"

"Not really," Lex said. "More, I'm wondering why Naline took a gun which presumably she knew was uncharged."

Delvia gave him a look of amazement. After a moment it yielded to relief. "Thank you, Lex. Were you also told that she took care to be seen by four or five people with the gun, and no one bothered to ask what she was doing with it?"

"No, but I'm not surprised." Lex moved to the handtruck and sat down on the corner of it. "I think I should have asked for your side of the story earlier. Tell me now."

She hesitated. Then, with obvious bitterness, she said, "You were right when you said I shouldn't come on your trip. I am impulsive, and never in my life have I had to restrain myself, so I don't have the habit. I'm pretty much what you might call a natural animal, I guess. I have reflexes. It's easier to give in to them than fight them, and it's more fun."

Lex nodded. "But you must learn how, Delvia. For all our sakes including yours."

"Oh, I know, I know," she said wearily. She dropped to her knees on the hot sand. "If I'd known what I was getting mixed up with . . . Listen, I'm not the motherly kind. I don't think I have an ounce of maternal instinct. And here was this gang of biddies squabbling over Naline, all wanting her as a kind of walking babydoll, with Ornelle slavering at the head of the rest. Naline hated the idea of letting them treat her as a kid. She wanted to think of herself as independent. Grown-up. Of course, she's not. She's a self-dramatizing, greedy, clinging adolescent. I wasn't fussing over her like a hen with one chick, so she attached herself to me. That was all, at first.

"Then it got really cold. Remember what it was like in midwinter?" Her voice was low and fierce. "Well, one night there she was, climbing under my blanket with me, *stiff* with cold. I know what I should have done—oh, yes! I knew my reflexes were set to detonate. I ought to have given her my blanket and gone out in the snow to cool off. Well, I didn't. Shivering in my sleep with a pitch-black storm outside, I wasn't in a state to think about noble gestures. And when she got warmed up enough to move around, well, what in all of space was I expected to do with her hands all over me and her tongue in my ear?"

She slapped her thigh with her open palm. "But I tell you this! If Ornelle or anybody says she could have done different, it's a lie."

"Go on," Lex said in a neutral tone.

"Thanks, I'm going to! Since I'm setting the record straight, I might as well make a proper job of it. Look. I'm a long way from my adolescence and I never had one like Naline's anyway, so it took me a shamefully long time to figure out what was attaching her to me. She's never seen me, Delvia-as-is. She's invented a Delvia that never was, sweet and generous and big-sisterly and so on in quantities enough to justify the way she throws herself at me. Why do you think I've been taking men like—like trophies even when it was still so cold it was damned uncomfortable and no fun at all? I've been trying to smash this nonexistent Delvia, get Naline to notice the real one!"

"Did you tell her to come out here and work with you today?"

"I did not. I don't give her orders. I didn't tell her

to go away either, though. I've been hoping she'd recover from her hysteria. But she hadn't. She tried to pick a quarrel, and I kept calm, and she accused me of hating her and snatched up a gun and ran off. I didn't chase her. I didn't think she could do any harm with it. It had been given to me as expended, for recharging. Lex, I swear I didn't know there was enough power left in it even for a flash discharge!"

Her face was pale; her lips were trembling. Lex looked at her for a long time. At last he said, "Go and talk to Jerode, Del. Ornelle's had a breakdown, and she's said a lot of things that'll make him readier to listen to you. Between you, you may be able to figure out how to prevent you being lynched when the news about Naline gets around."

◇ XI ◇

The little expedition moved off at first light the next day—partly to get as far as possible before having to camp for the night, partly to avoid making a ceremony of the departure. Lex had walked two or three miles up the riverbed to reconnoiter, to a hill which gave a good view of the next several miles still, and knew the going was fairly clear to start with. But for this, he might have postponed their leaving. A wind off the sea was piling up the clouds which had been on the horizon yesterday, the sun was hidden, and as the clouds approached the land they began to be carried upward.

With luck they might not spill their rain until they were over the high ground inland, then move on before Lex and his companions caught up. But they spread a pall of gloom over the first stage of the trip. Once or twice they had to use handlights even though dawn was long past. At least, however, it wasn't raining.

The people they were leaving behind might have been more pleased if it had been. It would have meant fresh water for washing, as well as the scant ration for drinking provided by Aldric's solar stills . . . which in any case could not last long unless the sun came back.

The contrast with the going at the end of last summer was amazing. This time it was far tougher. Newly-sprouted plants of all kinds fringed the river and a net-work of roots meshed out from the banks. The disappearance of the water had left them dry and fibrous, and the rotting bodies of freshwater animals were piled in what had been the last puddles. At first there were stands of quite tall timber on either side—trees twenty to fifty feet high, draped with an incredible tangle of creepers, vines, and plants for which no names had yet been invented. The river narrowed and its course grew steeper; then the trees were replaced by sucker-rooting shrubs only half as high, but equally festooned with creepers.

The mud had dried out and gave a good footing. They made fair progress throughout the morning. Around them were strange noises: oddly-shaped birds, yellow-gray and brown, shrilled and boomed, carapaced insects hissed and stridulated, and sometimes there were bubbling grunts which suggested that some large creature had been taken by what passed for its throat and was being strangled.

Lex and Baffin took turns to lead, their energy guns at the ready. Lodette was walking next, her bright eyes darting from side to side, warning them out of her specialized knowledge when they approached poisonous growths such as blisterweed or halting them cautiously when she spotted something not previously encountered. Now and then she used up one of the irreplaceable cubes for their only camera. More than five hundred had been rescued from the ship, but almost all had already been expended by Bendle's team.

Zanice and Aggereth, both apprehensive, followed her, and Minty and Aykin walked companionably at the rear, Aykin toting the heavy radio and accumulator on his broad back.

It was nearly noon when one of the unpleasant bubbling grunts broke from a few yards away, and they stopped dead on seeing branches flail as though a monster were thrashing about in the shrubs. Lex heard Aggereth's teeth chatter for a second before he clamped them firmly together.

Gun in hand, he advanced to the side of the riverbed.

Over his shoulder he said, "Lodette, we haven't run across any big carnivores, have we?"

"No. And the environment typically wouldn't support any. A beast over say fifty pounds' weight would be too heavy to be arboreal among such thin branches, and too bulky to move fast through this undergrowth. You'd expect to find the big carnivores in savannah-type country."

"Then what's that?" Lex said, and was surprised to hear his voice steady.

Peering out of the mesh of vines and creepers less than ten feet from him was the head of an animal. It was identifiable as a head only because of its gaping mouth; evolution here had not elaborated so many organs out of the basic gastrula as on most human-occupied planets. The hide was mottled. On a jointed neck the head weaved from side to side.

"That's—uh . . ." Lodette had to pause and swallow. "It's a herbivore, Lex. I've seen a couple of them back home. They got at our salad-trees. But we had no trouble scaring them off."

The mouth closed, opened; the head tilted skyward. The bubbling grunt repeated—and Lex slashed the beam of his gun down, across, and around. Vegetation shriveled, jerked back as though the branches were springs in tension. A waft of stinking smoke curled up.

"There's your carnivore," Lex said softly.

On the ground crouched, or squatted, or simply rested, a thing like a soft black bag, mouth uppermost. It was closed around the hind end of the herbivore, sucking at it, eroding it, dragging it down.

They watched with horrified fascination. It seemed impossible that the black bag, big though it was, should engulf the herbivore, which was about the size of a pony. Yet it was doing so. Now, with a sudden plop, the herbivore vanished completely.

"The damn thing must live in a burrow!" Lex realized. "That's only its mouth!"

"Lex! Watch out!"

The cry came from Aykin, standing five yards to the rear. He dived forward. But Lex, whose reflexes had been sharpened artificially like many other of his talents, had needed only the noise of a pebble falling into the riverbed to alert him.

Inches in front of his feet, almost masked by mud, dead weeds and intertwined roots, another black bag was opening. Its movement cracked off the disguising mud. It gaped, shut again, then opened to an incredible diameter, almost four feet, so that Lex could see down into it. Its interior was lined with ferny villae, hanging limp.

He said thoughtfully, "It looks as though this thing needs to drink as well at eat."

"You mean—you mean these are both part of the same creature?" demanded Aggereth, aghast. "Then it may run right under where we're standing!"

"Quite possibly," Lex agreed. "This is a hazard I hadn't anticipated. Well, we'll just have to be more careful. Lodette, do you see any complex of characteristic signs we can watch out for?"

The biologist bit her lip. She turned around slowly, surveying the neighborhood. While she was making up her mind, the black bag in the riverbed—still vainly gaping for water—rose questingly upward until its rim was a yard high and marked the earth like an ulcer. A thick nauseating stench erupted, and gases bubbled underground.

"Yes, there you are," Lodette said suddenly. She pointed to a lush-looking bluish-green stalk with heads on it remiscent of asparagus. "That's a plant the herbivores are very partial to. Usually they eat all the buds they can reach. But here, you notice, they're growing right down to ground level, with only a few patches browsed clean."

"They eat it where they aren't eaten themselves, is that it?" Minty said with a wry smile. She was holding Aykin's muscular forearm with both hands.

"Exactly. Where these shoots are common, we can be fairly sure we ought to walk warily."

"Excellent, Lodette," Lex approved. "All right, let's move on."

"What about the—the thing?" Aggereth said, gesturing at the black bag.

"It's dying without the water from the river," Lex said. "There's no point in doing anything about it."

But around the next bend what they had been expecting happened. The greenery walling the river closed in, and they were faced by' the mouth of a dim greenish tunnel. Lex sighed, and on glancing around was met with looks of dismay.

"It's far worse than it was last year," Baffin said.

"Yes, it is." Lex looked up at the sky. The clouds were

darkening, and though the rain had held off so far he felt it might break any time. He came to a decision.

"We'll rest here," he said. "Make a ring and keep a lookout over each other's shoulders. Break out rations and remember we may have to stretch them later on. Aykin, while we're still this close to the town, I think it would be a good idea to talk to Elbing."

The party made no attempt to hide their relief. They set down their burdens and stretched gratefully. Only Aykin, staring at the tunnel of foliage, didn't at first respond.

He said, "Lex, do you really think we're going to find the river's been blocked by a landslip, as we've been assuming?"

"It seems the likeliest explanation," Lex answered.

"Yes, but look how dense those plants are. Isn't it possible the roots make such a tangle they choke the stream? That would account for the flow recommencing at the end of summer when the vegetation dies down."

"Possibly, but I don't think so," Lex said. "They'd have to grow at a fantastic speed to cut the flow from normal to nothing in a little over an hour, which is what happened."

"Besides," Lodette said, "if this were a regular seasonal occurrence, that carnivore on the bank would be adapted to it. Instead, it seems to be dying without water."

"Yes, of course," Aykin said, and set about rigging the radio.

"In fact," Lex continued, "I think I know where the landslip probably happened. Baffiin, do you remember where the river cuts the edge of the plateau?"

"Where we had to scramble among all those rocks and boulders? Yes, of course. The banks are pretty high there. Do you think we'll find the water's backed up behind the blockage, or would it have found a new course by this time?"

"I hope it's found a new course," Lex said. "That much water backing up into a lake would probably drown the other party's site completely."

"Ready for you, Lex," Aykin said. Hefting the antenna-weight and aiming carefully, he tossed it into the top of the tallest tree near them. That was only fifteen feet or so above ground, but at this short range it should suffice.

It did. The signal was very clear, although faint—being intended for orbit-to-ground communication the transmitter was designed for a more effective power-source than one GD accumulator. Lex summed up their morning's progress and described the "tunnel" into which they would now have to plunge.

Elbing acknowledged the information laconically and passed on good wishes from Jerode.

"How's Naline?" Lex inquired.

"Better, I hear. But feeling's running high. The doc posted a notice giving his view of the facts—all about how she knew the gun was uncharged, so she can't have been serious and just wanted to attract attention, and so on. It's a pretty unpleasant business, though."

What would they find when they got back? Hysteria? Demands for a trial? A lynching? Lex didn't like to think of the possibilities. He made to sign off.

"How's the weather?" Elbing inquired.

"Rain's held off so far," Lex told him. "With luck—"

At that exact instant, a crackle came from the radio. He glanced toward the hills, then jumped up. Yes, the dark clouds were piling on the high ground now; he saw lightning like threads of silver wire sewing across their cushiony surface. Very distantly, the rumble of thunder followed.

Squatting on their bedrolls, they made their meal a hasty one. As he brushed the last crumbs from his upper lip, Baffin said, "Lex, there's something I've been meaning to ask."

"Uh-huh?"

"If the other party are dead, what's most likely to have killed them? Simple exposure?"

"I'd imagine so, Zanice?"

"Oh, yes. We didn't get off so lightly ourselves, remember. Think of Elbing's leg."

"It could just as well have been disease," Minty put in. "Or eating the wrong kind of local food. I don't believe they had as many diet-synthesizers as we do, did they?"

"Nor the people who could alter them to make antallergens and stuff," Baffin confirmed. "In fact we all tried to persuade them to come down to the town with us, because there weren't any decent resources handy. No timber within miles, some fresh water but not so much as we have—had!—just bare rock... But they insisted they'd rather stay put."

"Well, they arrived here the way we did, practically suffocating," Lex pointed out. Having finished his chunk of synthesizer cake, he linked his hands around his knees and rocked back and forth. "So they can't have had much time to plan their landing. Putting down on barren ground on a new planet has a lot to be said for it, though—you aren't immediately concerned with alien plants, animals, and poisons. And the only technically-trained people in Gomes's group were grounded in disciplines which weren't going to be very useful, like engineering. On the other hand I think Baffin has a good point. Once they knew that we had a doctor with us, and an experienced biologist, it was foolish of them not to trek downstream to our site. Granted, it would have meant a huge extra strain on our facilities, but it would have meant a lot of extra workers, too."

"I think they were downright stupid," Baffin said. "In fact I told them so. I mean, if they were afraid to put down anywhere but on bare ground, they might at least have picked a smooth patch of desert somewhere, with a good clean aquifer under it. It was courting disaster to choose a little rocky plateau so far above sea level."

Aggereth stood up, shrugging into his pack. He said harshly, "It's a bit academic, isn't it? Talking about the rights and wrongs of their decision, I mean! After all, we're on our way to rob their grave."

"You're right," Lex agreed. "OK, let's move."

◆ XII ◆

Through the enclosing tunnel of vegetation they moved steadily onward. Lex frowned on seeing how dense the plants were right to the bank and overhanging it. He had allowed an extra day for the return trip, but it was beginning to look as though that had been a grave underestimate. Either they'd have to be content with a mere inspection of the other party's site, instead of a thorough search for salvageable items, or they'd have to stretch out their rations for the additional day. Coming back they would not be climbing as they were now—they had reached steeper going—but traveling downhill would be no advantage if they were forced to chop a path at every step.

Animals moved in the undergrowth; occasionally things moved on branches spanning the river, with a scratching of clawed feet. Once he flicked up his gun and let go a single flaming bolt, and a creature with six symmetrically distributed legs and a pincushion body fell ahead of them. From the middle of its underside hung a long elastic tentacle tipped with a gummy ball. Lodette confirmed his spur-of-the-moment deduction that it must be a snare for prey, though she doubted whether it would harm a man unless the sticky ball was poisonous. No one was inclined to put that to the test.

They had agreed to make the best possible distance this first day. Accordingly they did not halt promptly at sunset, but continued with handlights. But the strain of scrambling over the loose rock that here filled the riverbed, often climbing more than walking, grew too much.

"Enough's enough," Lex said finally. "Let's clear a campsite, shall we? This looks like as good a spot as any. Baffin, burn the vegetation back a bit. The rest of you stand aside—we don't want to scorch you."

The others obeyed. With scything blasts of their guns Lex and Baffin shriveled the cover for a distance of fifty yards on all sides. The stench was foul, but lasted only a few minutes.

They made a fire of dry roots and heated soup to drink, then worked out a watch-rota and settled, exhausted, on their bedrolls. Except for an occasional animal cry, it was very quiet. Lex, who had ceded the first watch to Minty, thought as he lay down that one might almost call it peaceful.

But suddenly Minty let out an exclamation. Roused from the brink of slumber, everyone sat up in alarm.

"Water!" she cried, playing her handlight on the ground. "Look!"

Brownish trickles were coursing over the pebbles and mud. Aggereth climbed feverishly to his feet.

"If that's the river coming back, we have to get out of here fast! We might drown!"

"But it's not, and we won't," Lex said, after a careful study of the flow. "It's the first effects of that storm ahead.

We'll be OK so long as we don't lie down on the lowest parts of the riverbed, even if they are the smoothest."

With a snort of annoyance Lodette, who had picked a flat expanse of dried mud that must have represented the site of a late puddle, moved her gear to a safer spot.

"Think I should contact Elbing?" Aykin said. "So they're ready for this when it reaches them? A little rainwater would be better than nothing."

Lex shook his head. "It won't get as far as the coast. It'll be absorbed by the dry ground."

"Are you sure?"

On the point of saying—snappishly because he was tired —"Of course I am!" Lex hesitated. With a stir of surprise he realized: *Yes, I am sure. Because I'm beginning to get the feel of this planet. Like that creature with the sticky ball underneath. I never saw anything like it before. But I knew somehow what it had to be.*

Amazing. He gave Aykin a crooked grin. "Yes, because if I wasn't I'd move my bed, wouldn't I? Now get some rest."

He was right. By morning only a few damp patches acknowledged the rain as they continued doggedly upriver. Now it was definitely "up"; they came to long rapids and little sharp falls, and they began to see clear sky overhead for a hundred yards at a time as the vegetation thinned. While breakfasting they had spoken with Elbing, who told them Jerode had intended to talk to them this morning but was still asleep after a disturbed night. Ornelle had had another bout of hysteria, and someone in the single women's house had filled Delvia's bed with blisterweed, causing a tremendous row.

It took one person to set the example, Lex thought as he picked his way over treacherous pebbles, and there they all were behaving like children. Damn Naline!

At midday they were in striking distance of their goal. They occasionally glimpsed the highest rocks in the neighborhood of the plateau, and once Lex saw a gleam of sunlight reflected on what might—or might not—be the hull of the starship. But they had not yet come to the blockage in the river, and everyone was now staring ahead, rather than looking constantly to all sides, as though expecting momently to see the dam. He had to remind them to keep up a proper lookout.

Then he sighted a flat-topped boulder, almost cubical

and thirty feet on a side, half sunk in the soft ground at a bend. It would make a good place to break for the noon rest. Gratefully everyone scrambled up the smaller rocks around it to lay their burdens down on its flat top.

Aykin rigged the radio. Munching his ration of synthesizer cake, Lex heard Elbing acknowledge the call through the usual daytime mush of solar static, and ask for him because Jerode wanted to have a word.

"Doc," Lex said, "how are things going?"

"Badly," was the short reply. "Have you located that landslide yet? It's hot again down here today, and we need that water back urgently. The stink of our sewage alone is enough to drive you crazy."

"No, we haven't found it," Lex admitted wryly. "And we're almost in sight of the plateau. It must be right up where we suspected, close to the other landing-site. We may reach the place this afternoon if all goes well, but it may not be until tomorrow that we can tackle the blockage."

"Do your utmost," Jerode said. "Lack of water is just compounding a situation that's explosive enough without it. I've saved the sight of Naline's right eye, but her left needs a new cornea and I can't do anything about it with the resources I have. Should have started an organ-bank last winter instead of burying our bodies intact, I guess, but there was just so damned much else to do. . . . Did Elbing tell you what happened to Delvia last night?"

"Yes."

"Well, I'm inclined to accept Delvia's version of the background, but the fact stands, most of the other women are hostile to her, and Nanseltine came to me this morning all puffed up because a gang of them appealed to him to get her put on trial. I've no idea what sort of offense she could be charged with—I don't think there's one in the Unified Galactic Code—but that won't stop them. They'll invent something." Disgust clearly came over in his voice, despite the interference. "And of course too damned many people are standing around wringing their hands. The whole of Cheffy's crew, to start with."

Lex bit his lip. He saw Baffin frown, and Minty and Aykin exchange worried glances. On the off-chance that they might have constructive ideas, he looked an invitation at them.

"That Manager Nanseltine!" said Minty, and spat over the edge of the rock on which they were grouped.

"Not so much him as his wife," Zanice corrected in her quiet voice. "I know. The doc has sent me around to answer their calls—for a scratched finger or a bruised shin, they take to their beds, and they think every little headache is due to some fatal disease. I've seen how their setup operates. If there was any hope of getting them involved in something that useful, I'd say Lex should recruit them to his salvage team and quietly tip the boat over a mile from shore."

Baffin chuckled.

"No suggestions from this end, Doc," Lex said to the radio. "We'll just go find that blockage and let you know how soon the flow is likely to resume. OK?"

"Make it soon, please. Someone will be standing by here night and day." A pause; then, faintly as though picked up by accident, "What does *he* want? . . . Oh, tell him I'll be out in a moment!"

A sigh, and more loudly: "Lex, Rothers is after me now. I'll have to go. Do your best for all our sakes, and get back as quickly as you can."

They were very silent as they finished their food and gathered their equipment to move on. The blue-white sunlight felt suddenly oppressive and cold.

Baffin was leading on the next stretch, with Lex bringing up the rear. Now the vegetation had thinned to mere scrub, there was less need for watchfulness, but they could progress no faster because every few hundred yards was a dry falls, a wall of friable rock six, ten, or twenty feet high, up which they had to clamber on exiguous toeholds.

Encountering one of these, about eight feet high, Baffin prepared to do as usual. He poised himself before it, flexed his lean legs, and sprang up to get his arms and the upper part of his body over the brow. He hung there for a second, staring at something out of sight of the rest of the party, and then instead of levering himself up and over he fell back with a gasp.

"What is it?" Lex snapped.

"We've found our blockage all right," Baffin said, wiping his forehead. "Take a look for yourself."

Lex pulled himself up the rocks, swung his legs to the higher level, and stood up. Shading his eyes, he stared at what had so astonished Baffin. From here on, the river's course was straight toward the crags that fringed the plateau. A couple of hundred yards ahead, just about where he had imagined a landslide might occur, there was a wall. It not only blocked the riverbed, but extended a considerable distance either side, joining with natural slopes to form a continuous barrier. At its foot were high-piled heavy rocks; at intervals it was braced by wooden posts, and between the latter were what Lex judged to be hurdles of woven branches made watertight by plastering them with leaves and clay.

He was still gazing at it when Baffin scrambled up beside him and turned to help the others follow.

"What is it?" Minty called from below.

"It's a dam," Lex said harshly. He went on studying it. At the sides of the riverbed there were two extra-sturdy posts, and the hurdles between them seemed not to be fixed in place, but only lashed, so that they constituted a makeshift sluice-gate.

But—! He took a pace forward out of sheer surprise. A glance to right and left showed him the approximate level the pent-up water would eventually reach. Making the most generous possible allowance for the strength of those posts and hurdles, this dam was simply not going to last!

Now they were all up beside him, exclaiming in amazement. Aykin was putting their common thought into words when the soft-spoken interruption came.

"This thing is man-made! That means—"

"Stand quite still, all of you."

They froze. From among the rocks where he had been crouching a man in a tattered gray shirt and brown breeches rose into view. He was burned teak-brown by the sun and his eyes were narrowed against the glare. But he held an energy gun, and it didn't waver.

"We were expecting you," he said conversationally. "Been monitoring your radio as you came upriver. All right, go and take their guns!" he added more loudly, and other men as sunburned as he emerged from their hiding-places.

"What do you think you're doing?" Baffin burst out. "You don't have any right to hold us up like—like robbers!"

"You weren't going to break down our dam?" the man said. "You weren't going to take away our chief natural resource?"

"Do as he says, Baffin," Lex ordered. He tossed his own gun to the ground.

"But—!"

"Do as he says," Lex repeated firmly. Fuming, they complied.

"Very sensible," the first of the ambushers approved. To his companions he rapped, "Hurry up, there!"

"I believe we met last year," Lex went on. "Cardevant —isn't that your name?"

"Correct." The sunburned man peered at him. "Oh, yes. I recall you came up with Captain Arbogast. Tried to talk us into going along with your defeatist policy, abandon everything up here and taking orders from you instead. I seem to recognize that man next to you, too." He gave a sour grin and holstered his gun; his companions were now in possession of all the newcomers' weapons.

"What do you think of it, hm?" he added, jerking his thumb at the dam. "Isn't that something? That's our reservoir, back of there!"

"Calling us robbers!" Minty cried. "When you've stolen our whole river from us!"

"Oh, you can have the spillage back when the reservoir is full."

"Sooner than that," Lex said calmly.

"Oh, you're very cocksure, aren't you? It'll be a long time, I tell you." He laughed. "And like I said, we've been listening to your base calling up. Just a short while back, didn't your doctor complain your sewage is stinking?"

"What's that got to do with it? The water will come back to us of its own accord. I'd say—hmm. . . . Well, I'd need to see the other side of the dam to be sure, but I estimate it'll break in three days, maybe less."

As though he had been struck in the belly, Cardevant snapped his teeth together and drew his breath in with a hiss. "You cheap little defeatist bastard! I'm not going to stand here listening to your sneers!"

He whirled, gesturing to his companions. "Get them moving!" he barked. "Take 'em up and show 'em to Captain Gomes!"

◈ XIII ◈

By the time they were hustled in front of Captain Gomes Lex was feeling actually ill. The amount of effort that had been expended here was unbelievable. And the decision to expend it was incontestably insane.

The river, whose source was among the unexplored mountains beyond this plateau, was now flooding into the basin behind the dam. It was plain how it had been built. The sides had been erected first, then piles of rocks had been dropped into the water for the builders to stand on while they drove the uprights, and then the hurdles had been lowered into place, lashed, finally coated with mud and leaves. It must have taken the combined labor of a hundred or more people working like slaves to erect such a large structure in so short a time. And it was definitely going to fail soon.

Like slaves, it seemed to Lex, was the right term. For as his party was being herded up the last few hundred yards to the plateau he had seen gangs of men and women, filthy and hunger-lean, sweating to reinforce the dam with a man screaming orders at them. On the plateau itself, at the edge of which the ship rested—like a squashed egg, Lex recalled dismally—one would have expected to see constructions of some kind, but not what were actually there: mere shacks of the same mud-plastered hurdles, set up like animal-stalls. There was a stink of sewage and smoke; there were open fires burning in mud-brick grates over which hung crude pots on tripods.

Dull-faced, men and women stared at the outsiders going past, and overseers howled them back to their tasks.

Around the ship a frame of timber had been erected; ropes dangled from it untidily. Lex had thought the work involved in dragging the uprights of the dam all the way from the nearest stand of tall trees remarkable; it was miles from here. But bringing so many big trunks! It beggared the imagination.

Under the hull, stones were being hammered in by weary, gaunt workers, and others were leaning on long wooden levers. A child about ten years old was beating on a metal pan to mark the rhythm of their grunting heaves. Clearly an attempt was being made to jack up the ship so that its crushed lower plates could be welded tight.

Lunacy! Lunacy! Lex clenched his fists. He had had a score of possibilities in mind when he wondered what they might find here. The reality was infinitely worse than any of them.

Face like thunder, Cardevant was striding ahead. Too horrified to contain himself any longer, Minty exclaimed to Lex as they were driven in his wake:

"Lex, they'll never do it before the winter! And if they don't make proper preparations, they'll—"

Cardevant spun around, so rapidly that Minty didn't even have time to flinch, and slapped her across the face.

"We'll get through the winter like we got through the last one!" he declared. "And if the weaklings die it'll be no loss, understand?"

"Hit my woman, would you?" Aykin said. He could move fast for all his brawn; even the weight of the radio and accumulator which he was still packing didn't seem to slow him. His fist traveled quicker than even Lex could follow with his eyes, and suddenly Cardevant was reeling backward to lose his footing and sprawl on the stony ground.

He was no danger, but the others were. Lex judged instantly which of them was most likely to use the gun he had taken, and made for him. Just in time he struck up the man's arm, and the bolt intended for Aykin went sizzling to the sky.

"Cardevant!" Lex rapped, catching the wrist of the man who had fired. "You'd better not let us come to any harm, understand? We have more than eight hundred well-fed and well-housed people, and you have half that number of starved cowed slave-laborers!"

"You dirty defeatist!" Cardevant blasted back, forcing himself to his feet. The word, Lex noticed, had apparently acquired what he classed to himself as political force. "Well-fed, well-housed, hm? What about thirsty?"

Lex just looked at him. After a few seconds his anger subsided, though his tone remained as harsh as before.

"OK, I guess I didn't have to slap your loudmouthed

girlfriend. But if your people are fat and comfortable it's because they've given up hope. We haven't. We're working to get off this ball of mud, working damned hard. And we're not going to let anything stand in our way, least of all you!"

Under an awning improvised from bedding, Captain Gomes sat on a stool made from the butt-end of a tree-trunk poring over notes made on scraps of paper. Clearly these people hadn't chanced on the river-plant used in the town. There was another man with him whom Lex had met last year, his second officer, Probian.

"Good work, Cardevant," Gomes said, leaning back as the seven captives were forced into a group before him. He was a gross man; he wore only shorts, and his hairy torso gleamed with greasy perspiration. He was an amazing contrast to the scrawniness of almost everyone else. "So these are the buggers who came to smash our dam, hm? Not willing to let anyone prove they have more guts, apparently!"

Lex and his companions stood in sullen silence.

"You haven't searched their packs yet?" Gomes went on.

"No, sir"—from Cardevant. "Didn't see why we should carry them up here."

Gomes chuckled. "All right, do it now. Come on, you —drop that gear!" He folded his arms.

Lex shrugged and complied. The others followed his example, and Cardevant and Probian moved to inspect the contents of the packs.

"We took their guns, of course, Captain," Cardevant said, reaching into Lex's pack. "They had one apiece."

"Seven guns!" Gomes raised his eyebrows. "And you took them with one? Well, that's a fair return on investment. And a radio too, by the look of it—right, Probian?"

"Yes, sir." Probian was going through Aykin's load. "With a GD accumulator in first-class condition. That'll be useful."

"Not as useful as the guns," Gomes grunted. If that was his honest opinion, Lex thought, everything about this place was already explained.

"Medical supplies here, I guess," Cardevant muttered, moving on to Zanice's pack. He took them out: a few tubes of tablets, some surgical dressings and emergency instruments, a jar of tissue regenerant, what few other items Jerode had been able to spare. "And—what's this?"

He held up a jar containing Bendle's synthetic antallergen, which rendered a valuable number of plants edible. It did look very strange. It was a coarse crystalline powder of a shade between lavender and purple—ground-up sea-salt tinted with a solution of the chemical.

The rest of the party looked to Lex for a lead. He said after a moment's reflection, "It's an antallergen. You can sprinkle it on a wet dressing and use it to treat inflammation caused by blisterweed." Which was perfectly true; the poison in the leaves was chemically similar to the substance which made native vegetation indigestible. He went on, "I imagine you have a different name for that. It's a trailing plant which stings when you brush against it. It looks very like—"

"Oh, I don't want to hear about your damned plants!" Gomes broke in. "We're not going to be here long enough to worry about them!"

Lex fell obediently silent.

"What's that you've got?" Probian said suddenly to Cardevant as the latter drew out a transparent bag containing green-yellow leaves. "I found one of them, too."

"Botanical samples!" Gomes roared, and burst into loud laughter at his own joke.

Reasoning, however, that if there was one of these packages in each person's gear, they must be more interesting than that, Cardevant opened the one he had in his hand. Unconsciously he licked his lips.

"Say, it's their rations!"

Gomes responded to that, hunching forward and laying his hands on the table. But it was Probian who sighed on seeing the synthesizer cake, and hastily started to unwrap the identical package he was holding. The cake was folded inside salad-tree leaves, which he looked at suspiciously.

"What's this for?" he demanded. "To keep the cake moist? Isn't it dangerous? You don't know what you might catch from it!"

"We never had that kind of trouble," Lex murmured.

Probian gave him a distrustful glare, but after a moment he threw the leaves away and laid the cake on the table. A few crumbs adhered to his palm; he licked them off.

"Got something else," Probian said. He was at Baffin's pack now. "Explosives!"

He produced four precious blocks salvaged from the starship's disaster box, designed to hurl an instrument monitor and a subradio bleeper well clear of a drive explosion or other catastrophe, which packed enough power to clear the river if a mountain had fallen into it. They were shaped; one could touch them off at arm's length without harm.

That they were here on the planet at all was a source of endless self-reproach to Lex. He had been so fuddled with oxygen-lack, and his head aching so badly as they approached this world, he—along with everyone else—had overlooked the possibility of leaving at least this weak little beacon in orbit until it was too late for him to calculate a firing-trajectory for it.

Those also were laid like an offering on the captain's table.

"That all?" Gomes said.

"Everything of interest."

"Pity. Still, it's a windfall. I wonder what else they have down there. . . ." Gomes rubbed his bearded chin. On Zarathustra it had been customary to extirpate the facial follicles; however, there was no reason to expect Gomes, a spaceman, to follow Zarathustran fashion.

"Eight hundred well-fed and healthy people," Lex said. What a fantastic mischance had overtaken the others, up here! He could see it all now. Lacking anyone capable of making rational plans to prepare for a permanent, or at any rate indefinite, stay here, they must have turned to Gomes pleading for not guidance but orders. But Gomes was a spaceman, and could conceive no other course than repairing his ship. Whether or not he realized it was impossible, he had staked everything on it, and he was long past the point at which he could have changed his mind. By this time, perhaps, it had taken on the force of an obsession, and a contagious obsession at that. Those who argued that repairing the ship was out of the question (and judging by Gomes's estimate of the value of guns there must be many) were being driven to work regardless.

Consequently nothing of any practical value was being done!

"Yes!" Gomes was saying. "Eight hundred people—but without a ship of their own!"

"How do you know?" The words burst from Minty.

"Why, you told us!" Gomes retorted. "We were fully

intending to enlist your cooperation in getting our ships
aloft again. Even if we couldn't fly all the way back to
civilization, we could at least put one or both of them
into orbit and beam subradio signals for the searchers to
home on. There are bound to be searches going on. Aren't
there?"

That was a question which had long been exhausted
down at the town. None of the strangers answered. There
was no way of knowing. When the ships evacuating Zarathustra fled they had beamed continuously—but they
were racing at such velocity to escape the nova, it was
probable that drive-noise would have drowned the signals out.

In any case, the nova itself emitted noise.

"And—?" Lex said.

"Well, we got our antenna back up when the thaw
came, and what should we hear but some extraordinary
woman moaning at the mike, announcing that your ship
was in the *sea* of all places!" Gomes uttered a cynical
laugh. "Oh, I'd have liked to see Arbogast's face after
what he said about my landing. It's a shame you didn't
bring him with you."

"We couldn't," Lex said stonily. "He killed himself."

"Faced with a spineless defeatist lot like you, I might
have done the same!" Gomes rapped. "Some of this lot
up here were ready to give up and make themselves at
home—like animals! But we put a stop to that soon
enough. Hah! We made them listen to that woman sobbing. It turned our stomachs. That's why we didn't answer. We weren't going to let idiots whose ship had rolled
into the sea ride parasite on what we'd paid for with
sweat and blood!"

"Have you been living just on synthesizer cake?" Lex
said.

Gomes blinked. Then he snatched at a flattering reading
of the question. "Of course! We're half starved. And we've
had sickness and frostbite and in spite of hell we're getting on with the job!"

"How are you off for trace-elements?" Lex pursued,
and from the corner of his eye saw Zanice give a vigorous
nod. "You don't have a doctor or biologist here, do you?
A diet-synthesizer is for emergency use. A man can stay
alive for about two years on the cakes, but after six
months he'll start suffering from deficiency diseases, and
the moment the hoppers are empty the cakes are nutri-

tionally worthless—just bulk. Eating them, you starve to death."

"Starve?" Gomes didn't seem to have been listening. "Oh, we're hungry all the time, but we're not starving. Look at what we can do!" He rose, and for the first time Lex saw his legs. His calves were bloated and discolored, and there was a rag tied around his left ankle. He limped as he came forward, eyes blazing, to point at the ship.

"We're going to lift that ship into orbit! We're going to power her subradios and signal for help! It's going to take a while, but we'll manage it! And then *you*, you defeatist devils—you'll probably take the benefit and give no credit!"

"Where's your grav-free cradle?" Lex said quietly. "Where are your fusion arcs? Where's the chromalloy to patch her cracks? If you use mud, she'll burst open, the same as your dam is about to."

"It is not! It's going to give us hydroelectric power! Hah—didn't think of that one, did you?" Gomes was almost crowing. "We're building the turbines and generators now."

"We built windmills," Lex said. "We had plenty of power all through last winter. And we didn't steal someone else's river to get it, either."

For an instant he thought Gomes was going to strike him, not that he was worried—the captain was so slow from malnutrition and exhaustion, he could easily dodge the blow. Instead, he turned his back, furious.

"Oh, he's lying! Shamed by what we're doing while they give up hope and resign themselves to staying here forever! Cardevant, Probian! Get these revolting defeatists out of my sight. Tie 'em up and put a guard on 'em. If I see 'em again today I'll burst a blood vessel."

◆ XIV ◆

"What can have *happened*?" Jerode said for the twentieth time. Tiredly, Elbing raised his head.

"Doc, do you have to keep on and on asking that? It's getting me down! Anything can happen on a strange planet! That's one of the reasons I preferred just to visit them—get back into space as soon as I could."

"I'm sorry." Jerode wiped his face and dropped to a chair. He glared at the obstinately silent radio. "Is there no chance that—well, that their antenna failed, or something?"

"You asked that before, too," Elbing muttered, and bent to rub his short leg. After a moment, he added, "Excuse me." Unstrapping the peg, he laid it on the table.

"Is it chafed again?" Jerode demanded, suddenly remembering his medical responsibilities.

"Hm? Oh—no, it's not that. The skin's hardened up nicely. You did a great job for someone who'd only ever read about frostbite amputations. No, it's more a kind of itch." Elbing grinned wryly. "Not even a real itch, a psychological one. It's because now I'm this way I can't pace up and down when I'm agitated. The clump-clump of the peg-leg drives me crazy."

Jerode forced an answering chuckle and went on staring at the radio as though he could will it to crackle into life.

"Doc!" A hesitant voice came from behind the curtain screening the doorway. Recognizing it, Jerode stirred.

"Yes, Delvia, I'm in here."

She came through the opening like a shy animal, glancing automatically over her shoulder. Her face was drawn and strained, and her legs were smeared to the thigh with the angry strawberry-rash of the blisterweed which had been put under her blanket. By someone. They hadn't found out who.

"I—I guess I've come to ask for sanctuary," she said, striving for a casual tone. "Doc, I can't spend another night in that house. It's like a psychotic ward now."

"Thinking of coming over to the men's house?" Elbing drawled. "You'd be welcome there OK."

"Elbing!" Jerode snapped. Getting to his feet, he looked Delvia over by the dimming light which hung from the middle of the low ceiling. "You're in pain, aren't you?" he went on.

"Now and then." She grimaced and raised one leg to rub at it. "And I've got these numb patches, too."

"Giddiness?"

"Not since—oh, around lunchtime, I guess."

"Did the ointment help?"

"Oh, sure. It helped a lot. But I got a fierce dose of this stuff."

"You certainly did. Nobody else has had it nearly so badly. And to think it was done deliberately!" Jerode clenched his fists. "I wish I could find out who's to blame!"

"Don't waste time trying. The ones who didn't actually do it must have approved of it being done. I wish I'd left Naline to their tender mercies. They'd have found out she wasn't the kid they thought she was soon enough." Bitterness stained her voice like the rough red marks on her legs. "How is she, by the way?"

"I'm keeping her sedated until morning," Jerode said. "I want to build up her strength a bit before exposing her to the shock of learning that she's lost an eye."

"What about your other patient?" Elbing put in. "I mean Ornelle."

"Oh, I can tell you about Ornelle!" Delvia exclaimed. "Now she's back in circulation, she—No, I mustn't say it!" She stamped her bare foot to the floor. "Doc, do you have any treatment for a vindictive bitch? Because that's what I'm turning into, and I don't want to be that way. I just can't help it, the way they're goading me. Though I know they can't help that, either."

Elbing was studying her thoughtfully. Now, before Jerode could answer, he said, "Hey, Del! Full of surprises, aren't you?"

"Am I?" She moved stiffly to take the chair Jerode had vacated, sat down, and crossed her legs so she could rub the inflammation again. "I know I feel like a stranger to myself right now, which may account for it. Doc, can you spare me a couch in the infirmary hut or something? I need some rest."

Elbing made a disgusted noise and turned his back.

"You too?" Delvia said. "You think Naline tried to kill herself because I drove her to it? Don't bother answering, I read it in your face. Just tell me this, though!" Her voice rose sharply. "How do you explain her taking a gun she knew wasn't charged? I'd already powered up three of them! She'd seen it done! She can read a charge-meter!"

"All I know is," Elbing said stonily, "I hate to see harm come to any kid, no matter how it happens."

"You . . . !" But, hopeless, Delvia abandoned the retort. She glanced at Jerode, shoulders slumping. "You see,

Doc? That's the attitude, and you can't argue with it. I guess the nurses feel the same way, so my idea of sleeping in the infirmary wasn't so good. I'd better go out in the brush somewhere, then. I have to lie down, or I'll collapse."

She made to rise. Jerode stopped her with a hand on her shoulder. "You sit there for a while," he said. "While I figure something out. And you shut up, Elbing. I believe Del's account of what happened, and you'll have to argue with me if you don't. You'll have to make allowances for him, Del. Lex hasn't made contact since midday, and we're worried."

There was a thud on the roof, and they all flinched. Then they relaxed, shamefaced at their own alarm. It must be one of the omnipresent fishingbirds, clumsy in darkness, dropping to roost. They had grown quite used to the presence of the human intruders, and some had even started to make themselves useful by scavenging garbage —though that couldn't be allowed to progress too far, or they might wind up thieving from the kitchens.

"He oughtn't to have insisted," Jerode said half to himself. "If we lose him, we—" He realized what he was saying, and broke off, but Delvia had been listening.

"Doc, there's something special about Lex, isn't there?" she said, leaning forward. "What is it? *I've* noticed."

"Uh—well!" Jerode licked his lips. "Well, he's our brightest and most capable young man, isn't he? He seems to have an instinct for solving problems."

"Just an instinct?" Delvia murmured. Jerode, to stop her pressing the point, rubbed his hands together and affected briskness.

"Well, now! I don't like the look of that rash. Come along to the infirmary with me and I'll give you more ointment, and I'll see if we can rig a bed for you as you asked. Elbing, can you listen out a little longer? I'll pick up someone to relieve you on my way back."

The one-legged spaceman nodded. Turning to the radio again, he idly twisted the power control. But there was no lack of current.

Lex and his companions had been herded into a shallow cove among rocks at the edge of the plateau, some distance from the ship and the daub-and-wattle sheds which passed for housing. Part of the reason for isolating them, he suspected, was so that the workers here could not see them and contrast their own famine-struck condition with the evident health and strength of the outsiders.

His heart sank still further when chains with locks on them were produced to shackle them together. Those formed no part of a spaceship's gear, and certainly would not have been allowed to take up space in the panicky evacuation. What was one to make of a situation where such things were regarded as more important than proper food, housing, clothes? The fanatical determination of a few must be driving the others by methods not seen on any so-called civilized world for hundreds of years. Where in the galaxy did Gomes hail from that he even knew about fetters?

As though the chains were unreliable alone, an armed guard was posted over them too. Until sundown it was one of their original captors who stared menacingly down from the top of a nearby boulder; then a lean young man with bristling hair and a broken front tooth took over, mounting a handlight on a post nearby where it glared down on their huddled bodies. No food was offered, nor were their bedrolls brought.

"Are we supposed to lie in the open all night?" Baffin demanded of the relief guard.

"It's no worse than we have to put up with!" barked the broken-toothed man. "And it's not healthy to complain around here, because it won't get you anywhere! Understand?"

During the last hours of daylight, being so dejected, Lex had spoken little, but he had thought a lot. Now, sensing overtones in the guard's words, he came alert.

Tentatively he addressed Baffin. "He's probably right, you know. Gomes is deliberately making these people suffer—most likely, in the hope that enough of them will die to let him and a few others get back to civilization."

"But even with a few people on board"—Baffin was quick to pick up his cue—"that ship won't fly again without repairs which can't possibly be done with handtools."

"Exactly," Lex said. The others moved a little closer, chains clinking, to join the discussion. "Which means that—"

"Quiet, you! None of your defeatist talk!" the guard snapped. They obeyed, glancing up. Another handlight was approaching, jerking in a way that showed it was being carried by a man with a limp. In a moment the guard jumped up.

"Evening, Captain," he said in a fawning voice. Gomes's gruff answer preceded by a moment his appearance around the rock, accompanied by Probian and Cardevant.

"That's better," he said with satisfaction. "In a day or two, they may even be willing to work for a living. We could use some healthy men with muscles. And the women will prove useful too—ours are getting bony."

"And we'll recruit more when a search-party comes after this lot," Cardevant said, grinning. "To see why they haven't had their river back!"

"I told you," Lex called. "We'll get it back when the dam breaks. About three days."

"Shut your mouth!" The guard jerked his gun. Gomes gave him an approving look.

"That's the way to talk to them, Hosper. Good night. I'll stop by at dawn and see how they enjoyed their night."

"Good night, sir."

There was a whimper from Zanice. Aggereth moved close to her and put his chain-laden arm around her shoulders. Lex waited until the sound of footsteps died, then addressed the guard.

"Well, Hosper? Are we right?"

Nervously the guard stared around him, while Lex's companions tensed as though suspecting he had gone crazy. But then Hosper leaned forward, laying his gun aside.

"Of course you're right! That maniac and his crew have reduced us to slaves. Why do you think he had chains ready for you? Chains, whips, guns—they're the language of our lives! I only cooperate because . . . well, I've got a girl. It makes it easier for her if I'm one of the—the bosses. But we've done everything we can by ourselves. If someone doesn't help us, we're doomed!"

"How did they grind you down like this?" Aykin demanded.

"How do you think?" Hosper retorted. "We didn't have anyone aboard who could exert authority except the space crew. I guess we gave them a rough time during the flight. There was a lot of panic, and Gomes did have to be tough sometimes. When we landed, we were helpless, hungry, half out of our minds with shock. Then when your party came from the coast we thought wonderful, someone's going to help us—and then the winter shut down before anybody came back. It was terrible up here. We had no shelter except the ship, and the power ran low, and we had to lie six or eight together at night for warmth, and even so people died of frostbite. It was pure hell. Gomes and his officers imposed their orders at gunpoint because tempers were running so high, and two men—the only two with real guts—they drove out into the snow to die." His voice trembled.

"I don't know if I was smart, or just a coward. I'm not really a spaceman, you see. I was his supercargo, more kind of a businessman. But I saw early that I had to stay on his right side or go under. I've been so ashamed of myself. . . . Still, it has helped Jesset. That's my girl."

He had to swallow hard to regain control of himself.

"All the way back to the Dark Ages in a few months," Lodette said somberly. "I never realized how lucky we were."

"Well, you've got to realize it now," Hosper insisted. "We must get away downriver, tell your people, get them to come back and get rid of Gomes and Cardevant and the rest."

There was a bleak silence. Eventually Lex said, "There are two difficulties. First, we had precisely seven guns. We brought them all with us. We had no urgent need of them down at the coast."

"Oh, no!" Hosper bit his lip. Then he went on eagerly, "Yes, but there are eight hundred of you, all fit and well, while we're just a gang of starving wretches. Anyway, no one would fight for Gomes except—oh—about twenty!"

"But against energy guns . . ." Aykin said slowly. "Are there many?"

"Same as you brought," Hosper said dully. "Seven."

"Could we reach a radio?" Lex inquired.

"Not a chance. Gomes and his pals live in the ship, and they don't allow anything as dangerous as a radio to be removed from it. Someone did try to signal you, but Gomes caught him and had him whipped until he fainted." Hosper's voice shook. "The spare guns are in the ship, too. All except this one and the one Probian has. He's guarding the pens. That's what we call the hovels the workers sleep in."

"But you have an idea," Lex suggested.

"Not much of one, but . . ." Hosper hunched forward. "Look. I've fixed to watch you the first half of the night. And Jesset's going to be my relief. Gomes trusts us both. He has very few people he thinks he can rely on, and of course having you here means doubling the night guards.

When she gets here we can burn your chains off with this
gun. Cardevant will have taken the keys to bed with him.
He always does. We might be able to overpower the guy
guarding the pens—it's Probian right now, as I said, but I
don't know who's scheduled to relieve him. It should have
been me, but I asked for this job instead. What I'd like to
do when you're free is wake everyone and tell them to
rise up against Gomes, but there isn't a chance of doing
that without Gomes and the others hearing and coming
after us with guns."

"No, that's out of the question," Lex agreed. "I like the
rest of the scheme, though. I'd suggest we quietly slip
away downriver for a bit, and hide; then one of us can
break the dam. I'll do it. It's flimsy, so we won't need
explosives. After that—well, we know the way and some
of the pitfalls. We can beat any pursuit down to the
coast."

"At night?" Baffin said doubtfully.

"We're going to have to," Minty said. "That's all there
is to it, isn't it, Lex?"

◇ XV ◇

A stone turned underfoot. They tensed, staring out into
the darkness. But Hosper whispered reassurance.

"It's Jesset—I know her footsteps."

The captives relaxed. The long hours of waiting had
made them stiff and tired; besides, it was far colder up
here on the plateau than down by the sea. They looked
curiously at the girl as she appeared beside Hosper in the
beam of the hanging handlight. She was a catlike creature
with an elfin face, black hair cut short, and bright black
eyes; she was very thin and her ribs showed below her tiny
breasts. Her only garment was a pair of torn shorts.

Hosper hugged her quickly and explained that Lex had
accepted their plan. Now it was necessary to cut the chains
and go and overpower whoever was watching the workers'
pens.

Jesset smiled, sharp animal teeth glinting. "Where do you think I've been this past half hour? Didn't you realize I was late? And what do you think happened to my shirt?"

She raised her right hand, which she had kept in shadow, and revealed that she was holding another gun.

"I didn't have a chance to talk it over with you," she said to Hosper. "But it just struck me, it would be much safer to do things the other way around. Cardevant was due to relieve Probian, so I went with him. I had to make love to him, of course." She pulled a face. "But it was worth it. He won't be any more trouble tonight."

"What did you do?" Hosper asked faintly.

"Strangled him." In an offhand tone. "Just enough to knock him out. Then I tied him up with strips of my shirt and stuffed some in his mouth. But he may work loose, so let's not waste any time. You take that side, I'll take this."

More than somewhat impressed with this harmless-looking but ferocious young woman, the strangers carefully moved their chains, trying not to clink them, so that they could be cut loose with the fewest possible bolts from the guns.

The plateau was eerie in the starlight as they picked their way across it, fearing that at any instant the sound of movement would come from the spaceship, that a light or a gun would be turned on them. But Hosper and Jesset had promised that Gomes and the others would be in an exhausted slumber—indeed, they themselves were apparently sustained by sheer willpower—and they reached the river without difficulty. There was no guard on the dam.

When they reached the rock-face beyond, Lex stepped aside.

"I'm going to wait here," he said. "You go about a mile downstream, where there's a clear spot on the left bank—you know the one I mean, Baffin? We made a halt there last summer, on our way up. I noticed it still isn't overgrown."

Baffin nodded.

"Wait until you hear the dam break, then move off. I'll rejoin you in about seven minutes. Make the best progress you can—I'll catch up O.K. I imagine Gomes will be too distracted to worry about us for at least several more minutes. I'm going to try to keep that mile between us all the way to the coast. They won't even see us, let alone get within shooting distance. It'll be tough going, I'm afraid, drinking river-water filtered through our clothes and eating salad-tree leaves when we find them. But we'll make it."

The handlight, its beam narrowed to a pencil, showed him a worried look on Lodette's face. He clapped her shoulder. "Don't look so miserable! You're plumper than the rest of us—you'll last out best of all. Right? Hosper, may I have your gun, please?"

Hosper passed it over. He seemed on the point of saying something, but changed his mind. Together with the rest, he faded into the dark.

Lex waited a while to make sure he was fully night-adjusted. His infrared vision had been improved by the technicians who had worked to make him polymath material, and he always saw more clearly than an unmodified human, but it took about five minutes to achieve full range after seeing by an artificial light such as the handlamp. Then he moved silently away from the river to a sheltering rock from which he could inspect the face of the dam in detail.

What their chances were of reaching the coast, he was not sure. If only they had been able to steal some food and canteens of water . . . But the provision stores were as closely guarded as the guns; so many attempts had been made to steal food, Hosper had told them, that Gomes had finally decreed a death penalty. No one doubted he would carry it out.

Lex was shaken by the enormity of the thing he was fighting. Until now he had known about desperate men reverting to the primitive only as an abstract, an idea he had been taught about that related to nothing in recent history. Now he had seen it become reality, and he was appalled. This might have happened down at the coast, too. Instead of assemblies to discuss their problems, they might have gathered to hear Arbogast promulgate new decrees about working fifteen hours to earn one cake of synthetic food, to see a recalcitrant whipped for arguing back. . . .

It was unaccountable that the sufferer in the image which came to mind looked like Delvia and no one else.

Time enough, he judged, for the others to get their head start. He could see the water behind the dam, still slightly warmer than the surrounding ground, like a fuzzily glowing coal misted by ash. He leveled the energy gun, using the rock as a prop for his elbow, and put a single bolt into the spot which he had selected as the weakest.

He did not wait to see if he had been correct. He knew it. He turned immediately and began to race down the riverbed a few yards ahead of the trickling water.

The mud sealing the hurdles was washing away; the mud packed between the rocks that supported the uprights was becoming wet, slippery, acting as a lubricant now. Timing the process in his head, Lex ran like a deer, never glancing back. Four minutes of bounding and jumping. Five. The weight of the water was shifting the hurdles, bowing them outward.

Six minutes—and Lex hurled himself out of the streambed to fall sprawling on the bank, crushing alien plants and unable to do more than hope he wouldn't encounter a strand of blisterweed, while the flood went thundering past. On the first waves were broken hurdles, sticks, leaves, flotsam of a dozen kinds. Spray lashed up as the unpent fury of the water plunged over its old falls and rapids. Stones ground on each other, crying like pain-crazed beasts.

A breeze was coming off the high ground behind him. He tried to tune his ears and detect whether there were already shouts above the rush of water, but he could hear nothing and he had no time to spare. In a world that seemed shrouded by mist, where bare ground was gray-dark and vegetation and anything else fractionally warmer was gray-pale, he moved into the river-fringing vegetation.

Another couple of minutes, and he had caught up with the main party. They had advanced only a short distance from the spot where he had told them to wait until the dam broke. He ignored their muttered congratulations, closed his eyes against the handlight beam, and thrust between them to take the lead.

"Keep that light away from me," he instructed. "I'm dark-adapted now, and I've got to stay that way until dawn. It doesn't matter how much noise you make—what counts is to cover all the ground we can. Lodette, watch for blisterweed and anything else dangerous. Jesset, let Baffin have your gun. He's the only one of us except me who's made the trip before when the river was full, so he'll have a margin of extra attention to spare for danger. Now come on!"

He plunged forward.

It was only a few more minutes before there was a commotion behind them, easily audible now that the main flood from the dam had passed and the river was flowing more normally. There were shouts too distant for words to be identified, and from the rear of the party Hosper called that he'd seen a gun-beam.

"Keep moving!" was Lex's only answer. But privately he was hoping against hope that Gomes would not become so frantic that he would tell his men to burn a path for themselves. It would exhaust the charges in their guns quickly, but it would give them an advantage of speed which might prove decisive. After all, they needed only to get within sight of the fugitives to finish them off.

It became a sort of nightmare after that, in which springy branches slashed at their faces and legs, sharp-edged leaves prickled and scratched, and animals which were infinitely alarming because unseen were heard scrambling among the undergrowth. Their throats became dry, their chests ached with gulping air, and behind them the noise of pursuit grew louder.

"Lex!" It was Jesset's voice, acid-shrill. "They're using their guns to burn a path now!"

He acknowledged the information by setting a quicker pace still, but that was no answer, and he knew it. It was out of the question to burn their own path—for one thing, they had only two guns, neither fully charged, and for another the pursuers would eventually reach the point at which the fugitives had begun to clear the way, and their work would have been done for them.

"Ah-ah-*ach*!" It had been going to be a cry of pain; willpower turned it into a mere moan. But it sounded like a death-knell. Lex spun around, remembering to shut his eyes and preserve his dark-adjustment.

"What is it?"

"I'm sorry, Lex." Aggereth, fighting pain to steady his voice. "It's my ankle. I put my foot in a hole. I guess I can keep going, though."

"Zanice!" Lex said. "Quickly—look at it."

A pause while her deft fingers moved over the injury. A sigh of dismay. "That's bad," she reported. "A serious sprain—muscles torn. It's going to hurt, Aggereth."

"It does already," he admitted between clenched teeth.

Now what to do? They couldn't abandon him; they couldn't carry him and maintain their speed. . . . This looked like disaster.

And yet—! Lex had opened his eyes forgetfully, and was staring around at the enclosing vegetation. Something teased his memory. Those shoots! Those luscious ones with asparaguslike heads on them!

"Zanice, can you do anything for his ankle?" he demanded.

"Well, I can bind it up. He'll be able to hobble on it. Or maybe we could break a tree-branch to serve as a crutch."

Where was the thing? Lex was moving from left to right, parting the lower fronds and peering at the ground. Here a sort of mosslike plant was widespread, forming a smooth, slightly spongy carpet, and it was very hard to make out details. He had almost decided that he'd have to sacrifice his dark-adaptation and use the handlight when at last he spotted it, and gave a low whistle. A huge one! Eight feet across at the least, *underneath* the mossy covering, but showing through it because it was marginally warmer than the soil. And not just one, but another, and another, like the scabs of a loathsome disease.

He said, fighting to keep his jubilation from his voice, "Well, at least you picked a good spot to have your accident, Aggereth. Baffin, take a look here."

He shut his eyes as Baffin moved up with the light, and said wonderingly, "But there are five—six. . . . Damn, how many are there?"

"Enough!" snapped Lex. "Aykin! Pick up Aggereth; carry him across the river—"

"Here?" Baffin interjected.

"Yes, here! Take a pole and jab the riverbed before you put your feet down—that sapling there will do fine. Make sure there are none of these traps on the other bank. Go a hundred yards along. Zanice, bind up Aggereth's ankle there. Go on, the lot of you. Wait for Baffin and me. We won't be long."

"What are you going to do?" Hosper demanded.

"You'll see."

The others, unquestioning, obeyed. As soon as they were safely across the river Lex began to claw down branches and throw them as an extra disguise across the traps. Baffin copied him.

"That's enough," Lex said at length. "They're coming close. Now we'll burn a short false pathway toward them, to make it look as though this is where we started panicking. Then we'll adjourn downriver."

The lights and blazing guns of the pursuers came nearer.

In breathless silence Lex and Baffin saw them approach
the end of the false pathway their own guns had burned.
They halted uncertainly and looked puzzled

"Keep moving, you fools!" shouted a voice—Cardevant's, hoarse after what Jesset had done to him. "They
must be getting desperate! Remember we have a dozen
guns against their two!"

Lex turned and sent a bolt into the vegetation a hundred
yards downriver—but on this bank.

"There!" Cardevant shouted, and the pursuers charged
onward.

The ground opened under their feet. Four—five—six of
them seemed to shrink suddenly to half their height. Those
behind stopped and shouted; those who were trapped
screamed in mortal terror. Out in the river, there was a
sound of bubbling as the buried carnivore drew in the
water which was also necessary to its metabolism.

The others pulled at the captives' arms, failed to move
them; they kicked away the disguising branches Lex had
spread on the ground and fired at the ghastly engulfing
black bags. But the prisoners screamed worse than ever.
One, wrenched free, had lost a leg to the gun-beam; another
was rejected as the carnivore writhed in agony, but was
already dead when his companions dragged him clear.

"I—I can't watch anymore," Baffin whispered, his face
white as death.

"Nor can I," Lex said. With the grim look of an execu-
tioner he turned and led Baffin to rejoin the others across
the river.

The moans and screams died away behind.

◆ XVI ◆

"I'm a fool," Cheffy said dispiritedly. "I took it for
granted that because Lex's party had failed to contact us
they must also have failed to get the river back. So when
it did come flooding down in the middle of the night it
swept away tools, prepared pipes—things on which we'd

spent a lot of hard work, then left lying in the dry river-bed."

"It can't be helped," Jerode said, looking around the committee table. "At least the return of the water has provided a distraction for our troublemakers."

"Meaning me?" Ornelle from the foot of the table. She curled her lip. Against his best judgment Jerode had given in to her insistence that she be permitted to rejoin the committee. She did appear to have recovered from her breakdown, but so far her contributions had been unconstructive, and she was taking every remark she could as a personal insult.

"Meaning me?" she repeated louder, when the others tried to ignore her. "What you mean is, you hope the river question will distract people from doing the right thing by Naline!"

"You've heard what I had to say about Naline," Jerode returned curtly. "We are discussing a different subject. Now, as I was about to say: several people are demanding an assembly to consider the return of the river and the disappearance of Lex and his party."

Fritch slapped the table, open-palmed. "Pretty soon we'll be spending our whole time arguing instead of getting on with our work! I'm opposed."

"I'm afraid it doesn't really matter whether we're in favor or not," Aldric said. "These few days without adequate water, the psychological effects of the thundery weather, all the rest of it—it's brought it home to people that what lies ahead isn't just a little hard work, but a damned hard life. A hell of a lot of tempers have come to the boil. Some of my best men are scarcely on speaking terms with each other. I think we'll have to arrange an opportunity for them to blow off some pressure, Doc."

There was a pause. Bendle said eventually, "What *can* have become of Lex's party? Could they have been overwhelmed by the water? I mean, if the blockage broke of its own accord."

"No," Aldric grunted. "If they'd already been trapped by it at the time they failed to call us up, then the flood would have been on us an hour or two later instead of in the middle of the night. Much more likely is that the radio's broken, or they accidentally shorted out their accumulator."

"Isn't it a shame we didn't force Lex to take Delvia

with him?" Ornelle said. "That would have been a perfect solution."

"I'd far rather you were lost!" Fritch snapped. "You're getting on my nerves, know that?"

Ornelle rounded on the big architect, flushing. "Oh, I'm not surprised you'd rather have Del than me, Fritch! I guess you're one of her customers, aren't you? How's she taking her pay? Are you building her a little brothel of her own?"

"Oh, shut up, Ornelle!" Cheffy flared. Jerode banged on the table as all of a sudden everyone started shouting at once. Ornelle leaped to her feet and planted her fists on the table, leaning forward with a glare.

"I will not be quiet!" she exclaimed. "I'm sick of all this get-you-nowhere chatter! All this garbage about 'must let the people blow off pressure' and 'goodness what can possibly have happened to Lex?'—it's turned my stomach. I know damned well what must have become of them!"

"Then tell us!" Fritch barked. She swung to face him.

"Where were you when the river started running again? In bed asleep, hm? I wasn't. I was out for a walk. I couldn't sleep for worrying about poor Naline." She drew a deep breath, and an unpleasant sneer crossed her face. "It wasn't cloudy any longer on the high ground. You could see a long way. There were flashes up where the river runs."

"So?" Aldric snapped. "Must have been lightning!"

"It was not. The storm was all over. What I saw was guns being fired. Some of the vegetation burned for quite a long time, a couple of minutes."

"What?" Hoarsely, from two or three throats.

"I . . ." Seeming to speak against his will, Cheffy licked his lips. "I came out when I heard the water. And—yes, I looked up the hill too, and I saw flashes. I did take them for lightning, but now I think back, I guess they could have been gun-beams. I'm not sure, of course. But they could have."

"*Thank* you." Honey-sweet, sarcasm flavored Ornelle's words. "I take it you were too concerned with your lost tools and pipes to give it any more thought? Well, I hadn't been careless like that. So I worked it all out. Why was Lex so eager to go to the plateau? Because he wanted to get our river back? I don't believe it!" Again she sucked in a deep, rib-straining breath. "What they were after was the other party's ship. They didn't contact us when they should have because they found it could be repaired. When they realized we'd come searching for them if there wasn't some reason why we shouldn't, they staged this little drama with their guns to make us think they'd been eaten by animals or something. They knew we'd be awake and see them shooting because the noise of the water would have woken us up. Now they'll take the other ship and get away!"

The paranoid quality of the fantasy she had erected had shocked her listeners so much that for a long moment open mouths and horrified expressions were her only response. Jerode was wondering at the back of his mind what provisions could be made here to confine and treat the insane, when he heard a shout from outside which made him more relieved than he would have imagined possible.

Ornelle was still standing, under the misapprehension that her revelation had provoked amazement and awe, when the cries became clearly audible.

"They're back! Lex and Baffin and all of them! They're all back!"

The air seemed to clear of something heavy and dark. They jumped to their feet in excitement. Ornelle alone seemed frozen, and Fritch broke the spell on her by saying as he pushed past her toward the door, "Now maybe you'll learn to keep your silly mouth shut, Ornelle! Come on!"

As the others crowded onto the verandah, she dropped to her chair again, laid her head on her arms and began to weep.

The double news—not only that Lex and his party had returned, but that there were after all people alive on the plateau and two of them had arrived with Lex—spread like an explosion. Cheffy's gang, picking up the equipment scattered when the rushing water hit the upstream site of their sedimentation plant, had been the first to see them— limping, filthy, scratched, Aggereth hobbling with his arm on Aykin's shoulder. They had come back to town, their work forgotten, and as the word traveled around the rest of the community likewise abandoned their day's jobs. Even Lex's salvage team, who were out at the hulk of the ship marking it up for eventual cutting—the tools weren't available yet but Aldric had hit on a promising new idea —came hastening back.

But it wasn't simply the general excitement which com-

pelled the committee to call an assembly. It was what came
to Elbing's ears, what he relayed at once to Jerode at the
infirmary where he was attending to Aggereth's ankle and
supervising dressings for the minor injuries of the others.

"Doc!" the spaceman said breathlessly, clutching the
doorpost to relieve the weight on his stump. "Is it true
that the others are trying to repair their ship and put it
into orbit?"

Lex, his face showing appalling weariness, looked up
from the chair where he was eating a hasty meal while
one of Jerode's nurses cleaned the cuts on his legs. "That's
right," he confirmed. "Ask Hosper. He was Gomes's supercargo, by the way."

"Then they're crazy," Elbing said with conviction. "Captain Arbogast told me what a state it was in when he came
back from his visit. It couldn't be put back in space without a month in a grav-free cradle. No matter how long
you slaved on it with handtools, it'd never lift more than
a mile."

Hosper, who sat holding Jesset's hand in a corner of
the room, was gazing about him with hungry eyes at what
had been accomplished here. It wasn't surprising that they
were both overwhelmed, Lex thought, after their weary
months of sweating away at useless tasks.

Yet no one knew better than he how much remained to
be done.

Now Hosper spoke up. "Are you a spaceman?" he demanded. And, at Elbing's nod, he went on, "Well, then,
listen. The underplates of our ship are all strained. There's
a crack that runs about three-quarters of the way around
the hull. The whole drive gear has been shifted on its
mounts. The—"

"Don't go on," Elbing said. "I'm right. They *are* crazy."

The assembly came together in the hot air of early
evening. It was immediately clear to Lex that the situation
had worsened during his absence. People were grouped
differently. The two factions were almost perfectly defined.
On one side were the useful ones, clustered about members
of the steering committee—lean, tired-looking, heavily
tanned, with a kind of serious intentness in their quiet
speech together. On the other side there was a totally new
focus. Nanseltine and Rothers were together, and Nanseltine's wife, looking very bad-tempered. She had been assigned to work on a project making soap from ash and

grease, and resented it although there was virtually no other light unskilled work to offer her.

That much was to be expected. What was new was that next to the Nanseltines sat Naline, half her face masked with a thick layer of yellow salve and a pad of dressing over her blind eye. Incredibly, there was discernible self-satisfaction in her manner, as though having attendance danced on her by the Nanseltines, Rothers, Ornelle—who sat on her other side—and many more people was a complete consolation for the loss of her eye. Lex had read in the history of psychology about self-mutilation to gain sympathy and attention, but centuries of advancement in education had almost abolished such pathological behavior. If he hadn't seen what Gomes was doing, he would have found it hard to believe that regression could be so swift and far-reaching.

Yet, after all, the basic individual was much the same. Only circumstances had changed significantly.

The group centered on Nanseltine added up to a larger total than he had expected, and when he thought back on what Jerode had told him—summarily, in the infirmary—his heart sank. If only he and his companions had had a chance to sleep themselves out after their nightmare journey . . . But wild rumors were circulating, and it was imperative to scotch them.

He found himself frowning over the absence of someone he had been subconsciously looking for. Delvia, of course. And there she was, coming shyly to the fringe of the crowd as far away from Naline as possible. A few people gave her nods of greeting. Silent, arms folded, she sat down apart.

There was a sudden buzz of talk centered on Nanseltine, and the former continental manager climbed to his feet, his face red, his voice when he spoke charged with hostility.

"Dr. Jerode! Since you're delaying the start of this meeting I guess it's up to someone responsible to initiate discussion. What we want is straight information."

White-faced, Jerode looked up from his notes. But Nanseltine plunged on before he could be interrupted.

"We've been told that the other party, instead of tackling these hopeless and unwelcome schemes for a permanent stay which have been imposed on us, have made a bold and brave attempt, in spite of crippling disadvantages, to get their ship repaired and return to the comforts and sanity of civilization."

A ragged cheer went up. He waited for it to end.

"We have it on the authority of someone invited by you yourself to join your self-appointed committee—who can hardly be charged with bad faith!—that you propose to play down, to disparage this important news. What impels you to this cowardly course, I don't know: whether it's your lack of enterprise, I might say of guts, or your reckless willingness to jeopardize our irreplaceable possessions—let me cite only the fact that the team you sent out under the young and inexperienced Lex departed with seven precious energy guns and returned with a mere two, plus a pair of deserters from the other party who represent extra mouths to feed, and moreover they lost a radio, medical supplies, and goodness knows what else, and of course let us not forget the hard work wasted when equipment for the drinking-water plant was washed out to sea. . . ."

He was going on and on, and a frightening number of people were approving his hysterical onslaught. Jerode looked dumbly at Lex, seeking guidance.

What was to be done? Hosper and Jesset were pale with anger at what Nanseltine was saying; should Lex call on them? Elbing was muttering to himself; would the opinion of a spaceman carry any weight with people in this frame of mind? Of the members of his own team, both Baffin and Minty sat with their faces in their hands, pictures of hopeless misery, and the others wore expressions of uniform despair.

No, it was no use trying to reach these people on a rational level. They wouldn't believe even a firsthand account of life as Gomes decreed it must be. They would probably shout Hosper and Jesset down; they'd argue that Elbing hadn't seen the other starship for himself, so he must be talking nonsense. . . . One couldn't any longer regard Ornelle as sane, and in a very real sense people like Rothers and Nanseltine weren't either. They still craved the adulation and status which they had enjoyed back on Zarathustra, which even there they had not truly deserved.

Against an immense burden of fatigue, Lex forced himself to his feet. He drew a deep breath and shaped words which rang across the assembly like thunderclaps.

"Go to the plateau, then, all of you who want to! And damned good riddance!"

◆ XVII ◆

The passion of his words startled the crowd into silence. Even Nanseltine, the flow of his vituperation broken, stood bewildered for a moment.

More astonished still was Jerode. He said faintly, "Lex, you're not putting that as a serious proposal, are you?"

"Why not?" Lex blazed at him. "Let's stop fooling ourselves! People who turn their backs on their one chance of survival simply aren't fit to live!"

"Jerode!" Nanseltine had recovered and was demanding the attention he had enjoyed before. "Jerode, tell this young fool that we have no time to waste on tantrums! We—"

And at that moment the thing happened which broke the fiddle-string tautness of the atmosphere. As always, a dozen or so of the ubiquitous fishingbirds were perched on nearby roof-poles. Now one of them, tired of thinking whatever thoughts occupied its roosting-time, spread its dingy white pinions and made a clumsy leap into the air. As it passed over Nanseltine it let go one of the gummy black cakes of excrement which were scattered indiscriminately on beach, rocks, trees, and houses.

The black sticky blob landed plump in Nanseltine's hair, and a gust of laughter like a rising wind swept through the audience as he spluttered and clawed at it to wipe it away. It smeared his hands, ran onto his forehead, clung to his fingers when he attempted to shake it off. In moments he had become the clown for the assembly, and all their tension was hooting away in one vast peal of hilarity.

Probably, Lex thought, he was the only person who knew that that laughter had been triggered by the single forced giggle he had uttered, reflex-quick after the event.

No. Maybe the only person bar one. He saw that Delvia

wasn't laughing. She was staring at him. When she noticed his eyes on her, she raised one eyebrow.

The anger drained from him now, and cool determination took its place. Now or never he would have to establish his ascendancy over Nanseltine, Rothers, Ornelle, and the rest—to make sure that so many of the others saw the literal stupidity of their ideas they would never again be treated except with the contempt they merited.

A moment when the chief spokesman of the useless faction was a figure of fun wasn't an opportunity likely to be repeated.

Out of the sea of laughter new words were rising— spoken first by Cheffy, Lex judged, and picked up by those near him. "Sit down! Be quiet! Sit down!"

He let the shouts increase until they were almost drowning the last echoes of laughter, and then spoke sharply, raising his hand.

"All right, calm down. I think that fishingbird deserves co-option to our steering committee, though. It knows nonsense when it hears it, and has no qualms about making the appropriate comment."

That produced another wave of chuckles and fixed their interest securely on him. He stepped up on the verandah and sat down on a corner of Jerode's table, one leg swinging, exuding authority in every way he knew.

In a confidential tone, as though appealing to the entire crowd for personal understanding, he went on, "Now there's something that we're long past due to get straight. There are always people who have their minds made up before they hear the facts. Back on Zara, or any developed world, it's possible to put up with people like that. One lives remote from facts most of the time anyway. There are a dozen levels of insulation, from automatic housing to disposable clothes, from food factories to air-conditioned resort cities, which are designed to keep facts and us apart. In conditions like those someone who dreams up impossible projects can generally be tolerated, because computers and people with greater common sense tell them they're making fools of themselves, which is up to them, but they're not allowed to make fools of anyone else.

"Here, though, we're sitting on the facts. And they're hard and sharp. Here, people who prefer fantasy to reality are a burden. If you've studied Earthside history, you'll know how they handicapped our species in the pre-atomic age, and how much faster we moved ahead once sensible people realized that their commonest trick was to mess around squabbling with other people instead of buckling down to the jobs that really needed doing.

"Look around this assembly, and you'll see for yourself how the same trick has been pulled right under your noses. We're stranded on a hostile, undeveloped world. Are we all putting our best efforts into making life tolerable, all working together as a community? I don't think so. Because right here in this assembly there are two clear factions, and one is digging its heels in to hold the other back."

In the center of the crowd a number of people—a satisfyingly large number—looked around uneasily and tried to adjust their positions so that they did not seem to be on a dividing line.

Well, that was a start.

"I guess you're wondering what makes me talk like this. Well . . ." Lex measured the length of his pause carefully. "A few minutes ago you heard Nanseltine dismiss me as young, inexperienced, unfit to head even a group of half a dozen people who cheerfully accepted me as their leader. I was prepared for him to say that, because it's one of the things they warn you about in polymath training."

He articulated the last sentence very carefully, so that no one would be in doubt as to what he had said. Even so, the shock took a while to be digested. He glanced around, spotting key reactions.

Jerode: pure relief, which might translate as, "He's come into the open at last!" Hosper and Jesset: "Small wonder they've achieved so much here, with a polymath to help them!" Nanseltine: naked horror at the extent to which he had made himself appear foolish. Delvia: her lower lip caught up between her teeth, and a thoughtful nod. Aldric, Cheffy, Fritch, Aykin, Minty, and many many others showing mingled wonder, relief and excitement.

It was inevitable that someone would challenge the remark. The one who did was Ornelle, clambering to her feet and pointing a quivering finger at Lex.

"You're lying!" she shrieked. "It's a plot you've cooked up with Jerode to cover up what you did to Naline!" She clutched Naline's shoulder convulsively with her other hand. "If you're a polymath, why didn't you say so before? It's a lie, a shameless lie!"

"I didn't say I was a polymath before because I'm not

one," Lex corrected. "I've had polymath training and incomplete physical modification. Let's just get it clear what a polymath is, because if you don't know I guess a lot of others here don't. A polymath is a man or woman adapted and trained for years, right up to the age of forty, to take on one job on one particular planet. Not a superman, not a kind of walking computer, just a person with a special kind of dedication who's been worked on by a vast team of experts, chemically, surgically, intellectually. . . . I couldn't tell you this, because you'd expect me to perform miracles. First you had to get acquainted with me as a person, didn't you? Otherwise you'd have regarded me as a machine.

"And there's another point, too. Even after he's fully trained, a polymath has to spend another *twenty years* on the planet he's been assigned to, getting to know it intimately, before he's left in charge. Uh—to put it mildly, this world was rather hastily selected for colonization."

Wry grins. He estimated four hundred of them. That meant he was bringing a full half of the community to his side now. Even so, he had to kick the rest along too.

"Now the polymath's job after this special training is to oversee the work of the first continental managers and stop them making idiots of themselves."

There. Lex almost winced at the conceit implicit in the statement, but it was essential. Nanseltine, still scrubbing at his face and hair with a bit of cloth, was making himself as small as possible, as though hoping to escape notice. He wasn't after Nanseltine personally, of course; he must, though, strip the man of his spurious claim to authority once for all.

"Among the most important things he's taught to watch out for is the risk of what's happened here—people dividing what has to be a united effort until the planet is finally tamed. I'm disappointed that *Manager* Nanseltine" —he loaded the title with bitter sarcasm—"isn't aware of that too. Maybe it's because he's never worked with a polymath."

The corollary, that he knew very well how to oppose one, could almost be heard clicking into focus in the minds of the audience. Next, then, he must dispose of Ornelle. He hated the calculated way in which he was planning this assault, but he knew it was economical of their most precious asset: time.

There was a prehistoric saying: "Needs must when the

devil drives." If there was a devil on this planet, it was in the minds of those who shut their eyes to the truth.

"That's not the worst division we're suffering, though. A much more serious one has cut us off from our fellow survivors up on the plateau. I guess a lot of you have been wondering why they refused to answer our radio calls, why they didn't want to work together with us. Well, the people who can tell you most about this are the strangers here, Hosper and Jesset, who came back with us. Let me put some questions to them."

Hosper rose, steadying himself on a torch-post. It was growing toward full dark, but no one had yet lit the torches. Lex whispered to Jerode, and somebody was detailed to attend to the job.

"Hosper!" he went on. "Captain Gomes told us why he'd refused radio contact. Maybe you'd like to inform everyone what he said?"

Looking tired to the point of collapse, the shock-haired man spoke in a flat unemotional voice.

"He had us re-rig our antenna when the thaw came, and we thought we could appeal to you for help against him because he's out of his mind, as you may know already I guess." The words followed one another with almost no stress or inflection. "But we heard some woman moaning about how bad it was down here and how your starship had rolled out into the sea and you were all going to starve to death and die of plague and like that. So Gomes got it into his head you were all going to come up and try to steal his ship from him, and he wouldn't let anyone transmit at all, not even to say we were still alive. I never could make sense of all that and now I'm here and I've seen the miracles you've accomplished"— life was creeping into his voice at last—"I don't even know if it was really someone calling from here or whether it was some trick Gomes played on us to stop us hoping."

"The call was from here all right," Jerode said, and the words were an indictment. He sounded vaguely astonished, as though he had just put two and two together. "I found Ornelle weeping over the mike of our radio, and I recall I had to tranquilize her because she was over the edge of hysteria."

Heads turned. All the eight hundred people looked at Ornelle, and the looks were angry.

"She was at it for going on three days," Jerode finished.

"You mean *she* did it?" Beside Hosper, Jesset was rising, pointing at Ornelle on whom all eyes were turned. Famine-thin, yet with a fire of hate burning behind her dark eyes, she looked like what suffering had made her: a wild beast. "It was because of her that we had to go on being whipped, starved, chained together? Not daring to lie down when we were sick for fear of being beaten back to work, threatened with guns if we rested for a minute? *Her* doing?"

For a moment Lex feared she might spring at Ornelle and serve her as she had treated Cardevant. He barked, "Jesset! On the plateau! Where do people sleep?"

"In filthy hovels made of mud! On the bare ground!"

"Gomes and his officers?"

"In the shelter of the ship!"

"How long do you work?"

"Dawn to dusk every day, sick or well!"

"What do you eat?"

"Synthesizer cake! Two a day!"

"What do you drink?"

"River-water! Boiled in clay pots on open fires!"

"If you refuse to work?"

"They make you work in chains!"

"If you're too ill to work?"

"They whip you until you get up!"

"If you can't get up?"

"They let you die!"

And then, suddenly, her face crumpled and she began to cry. Hosper caught at her, drew her down beside him with both arms, and pressed her to him. His words were audible to the entire gathering.

"You're safe now, Jesset! You're safe! You don't have to be frightened anymore."

When the following silence had become unbearable Lex spoke again, hearing his voice gravelly and unfamiliar.

"I suggest that we make available to those who want to work on spaceship repair whatever they need for their journey—issue rations, canteens of water, bedrolls, and so on. Doc, you'll organize that, won't you? And it isn't difficult to find the way. You merely follow the river until you come to the edge of the plateau. In fact you can see the hull of the spaceship from quite a distance off. I did think it only fair, though, that those intending to make the trip should be informed of what they can expect at the end of it."

He looked out over the assembly, That brief, bitter interrogation of Jesset had finished his work. It told the audience more with its ferocity than hours of detailed explanation could have achieved. People had scarcely moved. Yet there had been a withdrawal. Nanseltine and Ornelle, because they had been named, were—cast out. Even Naline had turned her single eye on Ornelle and was staring at her as though at a stranger.

Once, Lex reflected sadly, there had been creatures called scapegoats. Centuries later, parsecs distant, for the sake of the community he had created scapegoats anew.

◆ XVIII ◆

When it was over he felt drained of every ounce of vitality, yet paradoxically at the same time he was so keyed up he could not think of relaxing. A temporary solution had been found to the worst problem afflicting their community—a human one, inevitably; now, as though that had been fogging the foreground of his mind, a hundred other problems sprang sharply into focus. As the assembly melted away into the darkness, he sat slumped in a chair and stared unseeing toward infinity. His party had kept going all last night to get back to the coast, and the night before they had only snatched a couple of hours' sleep. Now he craved for rest, and his busy mind would not concede it.

Moreover, the committee members were gathering around him, a little hesitantly because the Lex they had known had turned out to be that improbable, near-alien creature, a polymath. Not all his careful disclaimers had rooted out their half-superstitious regard for those to whom the fate of a whole new world could be entrusted.

It dawned on him that they were grouping about him in a semicircle, waiting to be given orders. He spoke irritably, not looking at anyone.

"Before we go any further, let me make one thing clear. You are not going to come running to me with every petty little question that crops up, understood? You're all able men in your own right. You've done wonders here. If you haven't acquired the confidence you need to trust your own judgment, you're not the people I think you are. So, for instance—Bendle!" His eye fell at random on one of the group. "If you want me to tell you how to run long-chain structure analysis with three clay pots and a GD accumulator, don't waste your breath. I am not a magic box on legs, press a button, and out pops what you want. I've been tossed like everyone else into a situation I didn't ask for, I'm hardly even capable of feeling grateful to be alive because this is the wrong planet as far as I'm concerned, and I can get as angry as anybody else when I'm pushed to it."

The committee members exchanged glances. After a pause Fritch spoke up bluffly.

"Point taken, Lex. I guess all of us want to go on seeing things run by popular consent, too, not by one man the way they are up on the plateau."

"And I guess a lot of us didn't realize how lucky we've been," Bendle supplemented. "I felt bitter when my boy died. If I hadn't been too busy to sit and mope I could have wound up like Arbogast."

They were talking sense. Lex cracked a faint relieved smile.

"No, what we came to ask you about is the thing that's bothering a lot of people," Fritch went on. "That is, what are we going to do about the other party? Some of us are so incensed, they're all for organizing a sort of army and going up to set free the slaves. Of course Hosper and that little spitfire of a girl of his are pressing the idea on everyone they can get to listen. But as I understand it, they were coming after you with guns, and they'd cheerfully have murdered you if you hadn't lured them into this—this underground man-eater thing."

Lex didn't say anything, but gave a half-nod, letting his eyelids drift down.

"And it seems to me," Fritch insisted, "that there's a much more urgent question. Are the bastards going to come after us? I figure that so long as they believed the wild tale Ornelle spun over the radio, all about how awful life was down here, they didn't think we had anything they wanted. Now they've seen your team, Lex, and talked to you, and they know we only have two guns to defend ourselves with, aren't they likely to mount a raid, try to steal equipment and food?"

"Not tonight, at any rate," Lex grunted. "They lost too many men when we led them into our trap. Hosper says there are only about a score that Gomes trusts, and two died and I think three others must have been pretty badly injured. But you're right. We'll have to mount some kind of guard."

"And what are we going to do to help those poor devils?" Jerode muttered. "We can't ignore them!"

"No more can we raise an army in a single night!" Lex said with a touch of impatience. "Yes, we'll have to plan what we're going to do about that, and I'm afraid we're going to have to draft a formal constitution for ourselves, and figure out a way to prevent non-sane individuals from becoming a charge on the community, and make preparations for a flood of sick and starving fugitives, and— *and!*" He slapped his thigh and stood up. "But right now I'm going for a walk on the beach to relax before I lie down. I haven't slept for two nights and anything I say at the moment is apt to be so much wasted air. Good night!"

On the edge of the beach he paused. In the starlight the skeletal forms of the solar stills and boilers were like the bones of ancient ships half buried in the sand. Someone with an inventive turn of mind had rigged a gadget, powered by a float bobbing in the water, which at irregular intervals jerked a clanging sheet of metal against the main boiler to discourage fishingbirds from perching there and smutching the reflectors with their droppings. Out near the hulk of the starship luminous bubbles were rising to the surface. A sea-beast was feeding, releasing gas from the carcass of one of the sessile animals on the oceanbed. They had grown to an alarming size in the past couple of weeks, and it was a major job to avoid their reaching arms when working on the ship.

The bones of ancient ships. . . . The image took hold of his imagination and sent a shiver down his spine which had nothing to do with the cool wind now coming from deep water, flavored with salt and the smell of sea-life.

He had never admitted it to anybody, but he too— right up to the time when he realized what Gomes was doing—had been half hoping that it might be possible next year, or the year after, to lift if not a complete ship then at least a subradio beacon and a power source into orbit, let whatever searchers there might be know how far they had had to flee for survival.

Now he was cured of that vain hope. It wouldn't be done this year or next. It might not be done in his lifetime. For the first time he faced the knowledge squarely. Without clues to guide them, the searchers would almost certainly assume that nobody from Zarathustra had survived except those who left in ships that took off early enough to circle around the nova and head back toward the older systems.

Ultimately the tide of expansion would engulf this planet too—in five hundred years, in a thousand. What would the scouting parties find? A new branch of the family of man, its planet tamed, reaching once more to the stars? Or—

"Bones?" he said aloud. "Scraps of corroded metal? Bits of plastic buried in the sand?"

There was a sound of movement near him. Startled, he whirled, and a voice spoke from deep shadow behind the main boiler.

"Lex, is that you?"

"Delvia! I'm sorry, I didn't realize there was anyone—"

"Oh, I'm alone, if that's what's worrying you." She rose into sight. "I guess I'm becoming a reformed character. I spend a lot of time out here by myself, just thinking. Sometimes I sleep here."

"Just to be alone! If so, I'll move on."

"No." She kicked at the sand. Grains of it rattled on the nearest reflector, like dried corn spilling into a pan. "Mainly I come out here to look at Zara. It seems absurd that the star which I used to think of as the sun is still up there, shining quietly, when in fact it's a raging cosmic explosion. How long before we see it happen, Lex? Is it sixty years?"

"More like seventy," Lex said. Since the early days he hadn't often looked up to see Zarathustra's primary, soberly yellow like a thousand others, in the night sky. Now his gaze fastened on it automatically.

"So in fact *we* probably won't see it," Delvia said.

"No. I don't know if that's something to be grateful for or not."

"Not." She uttered the word positively, with conviction. "If we could see it, a great blazing sore on the sky, it would bring the truth home to us. It hasn't reached me, you know. Sometimes I sit here and look up, and I try to remember what it was like to live in a civilized, orderly, safe environment—and because Zara is still there I almost convince myself that that's the reality and this is only a nightmare interlude."

She glanced at him. "Do you agree with me, Lex, that that's half our trouble? That it isn't real to us yet? We're still playing, *I* think. Sure, we work to make ourselves less uncomfortable, to get food and water and shelter. But inside we're treating it as a glorified camping trip."

"Yes, I think you're right," Lex said.

"But being right—does that count for anything?" She sounded dispirited. "I never dreamed this might happen to me, being cast away on a strange planet, with no hope of getting back all the things one used to take for granted. It makes me feel like—well, a prisoner. A condemned prisoner, not guilty of any crime. Do you ever find yourself feeling that the universe has punished you unjustly?"

Lex hesitated. Eventually, in a low tone: "Yes, often."

"It must be particularly bad for you, I guess," Delvia said. "But you hide it so well. That's why I've always suspected there must be something special about you. Or am I wrong? Are you better adjusted to what's happened, because you've known for years that your life would be lived out under another sun?"

"Oh, no." Lex gave a little dry chuckle. "I've just got over the first impact of what you've been talking about, and it's been hard. I've been trying to make myself understand in my guts that what we do here won't be for our own sakes. It'll have to be for the children who are born in the fall, and their children—maybe. We're living in the past and trying to build for the future, and we have no present for ourselves."

"We've been hurled back to the deep past," Delvia suggested. "Not our own, more the days when savage tribes were first spreading across the face of Earth."

"No, there's no comparison. They weren't torn apart the way we are. They'd neither lost their own past, nor conceived the possibility of changing the future by an act of will. We're unique, Del. That's why our job is so hard."

There was a pause. Delvia began to walk away from the boiler, and unconsciously he fell in beside her, staring at the sea.

"Do we have any hope, Lex?" she said when they had wandered some distance.

"Of what? Of achieving our goal here, of getting a signal home and being rescued?"

"Any kind of hope. It's what we most desperately need. And we don't really have any. We're just pretending we have. If you can give it to us, we'll be safe no matter what else becomes of us."

He looked at her as though he had never seen her before. He said, "You've changed. Or—no, wait a moment. I wonder if it's we who are changing, and you got there a jump ahead of the rest."

"I don't understand you." She halted and faced him, one foot raised to rub the other calf. There were still traces of blisterweed rash on her legs.

"I remember thinking," Lex said slowly, "some time ago, that what we could do with was a lot more Delvias and a lot fewer Ornelles and Nalines."

"I'm flattered." She inflected the words ironically, but they sounded lifeless. "I'm sure I don't know why."

"Nor did I until now, but I think I've found out. You have a present. You live in the here and now, and that's why the rest of us are jealous of you. Being alive was enough reason, as far as you were concerned, to go on living when things got hard. I saw the way you picked a job for yourself, to do by yourself, while the rest of us were arguing till we were blue about our plans. And it turned out to be an essential job which hadn't even occurred to us."

"Is that supposed to make me a genuis, or something? Because I promise you I'm not."

"And you went on being able to enjoy living," he said as though she hadn't spoken.

"Did I? No, I thought I did. But what I got was a load of misery. Living in the present, if that's what I've been doing, isn't any fun at all. Besides, the future is what counts now, and that depends on you. . . . Lex, what's wrong?"

He was shaking suddenly, shaking from head to foot like a fiercely vibrating machine about to break loose from its mountings. He couldn't say anything. His teeth had locked, his fingers folded into fists, in his struggle to control and end the dreadful trembling. It was as though Delvia's words had made the whole immense burden of his duty solid and dropped it on his shoulders, so that he had to fight to remain standing. He closed his eyes and thought he might scream. Anything, to switch off his awareness!

Then she was saying his name over and over, "Lex, Lex, Lex, Lex. . . ." Her arms were around him. Dimly, through all the layers of his terror, he could feel her skin. She had slipped off her one garment; she was taking his hands and pressing them to her body and some archetypal reflex made them grip her flesh; she was bending his head to her breasts so that he breathed the warm scent of her.

When the shaking had stopped, she still said nothing but his name, and drew him down beside her on the sand.

◆ XIX ◆

During the days which followed the endless vistas of future problems more than once threatened to paralyze him with the same shivering fear. And if him, then how many others? For the first time he comprehended men overwhelmed by what had happened to them, shocked by calamity, strained to the limit of their endurance, nervous tension knotting their jaw muscles, drying their mouths, turning their stomachs sour, yet not daring to let themselves explode into aggression or rail at the circumstances which oppressed them. In Delvia's phrase: feeling that the universe had unjustly punished them.

It was worse for the men than the women. Imperceptibly their quasi-primitive predicament had reawakened the ancient habit of looking to the male as organizer and leader.

During those fearful moments on the beach, Lex knew, he had been balanced on the brink of insanity. He had found in himself that weakness which had driven Arbogast to suicide, which had allowed the refugees on the plateau to let themselves be dominated like beasts, brutalized without offering resistance.

But Delvia had realized what she must do. Might one say "instinctively"? (She had said—so long before that he felt he was recalling the words from a previous existence

—she had always been "what you'd call a natural ani-mal.")

No, not instinctively. From experience. Lex wondered, though he would never have dreamed of asking, from whose shaking moaning body she had first learned to purge the evil of terror.

He could spare little time now, though, to worry about himself. It was as though the universe had shifted to a different track with his assumption of authority. There truly was no present for the refugees, merely the illusion of one. The past had spewed them out, and only in the future could they justify themselves.

Indeed, their plight was unique. Who else in all of history had been compelled to found their present not on what had gone before, but on what was yet to come?

So, in this oven-heat of summer when the air shim-mered on the hills and the still sea gazed up at images of itself miraged on the horizon, everything said to him with-out ceasing, "Visualize! Predict! *Plan!*"

Immediate plans, contingent plans, emergency plans. Practice routines, normal routines, emergency routines. He could frame one plan and perfect it, and something would happen to undermine his careful scheme. That job required this tool, and with it could be done in a few days. Unfortunately this tool had been left on the riverbed and swept away with Cheffy's lost equipment. Was it quicker to evolve an alternative method, or replace the tool by getting Rothers to melt down steel in his solar furnace and have Aldric cast it, so that one of the women could file it sharp with a power-grinder borrowed from Fritch and driven off a solar collector sheet normally employed by Delvia to charge accumulators and then fit the blade with a wooden handle which someone else had turned from a branch, sanded smooth and bound with scarce wire against splitting, time invested one hour? The lack of the power-tool affected work on the new buildings, while the lack of the collector sheet might mean a shortage of charged accumulators and the need for more might crop up anywhere—in Bendle's lab-hut, out at the sedi-mentation plant, in the infirmary, *anywhere*.

Proof was all about them that Jerode had set scores of crucial projects in motion during his tenure. What Lex found most terrifying was that despite Jerode's work he never stopped thinking of new tasks, equally important.

And always, especially when he saw Hosper or Jesset

pass by but at any other time as well, his mind was clouded by the thought of the other refugees on the plateau, driven by madmen to waste their energy and possibly their lives.

But he was adamant that no attack should be made on the plateau before arrangements had been made for an influx of three to four hundred survivors, most of them sick or injured, all weak. Moreover, if—as seemed likely —toward the end of summer their overused diet-synthesizers began to break down, there would have to be food in store, enough to last until spring. In addition it was self-defeating to use power for heating only to lose it through bad insulation, and though their improvised windmills had worked amazingly well they would be inadequate for the enlarged community. . . . And there was an increasing number of married couples for whom Fritch was providing separate accommodation, only that absorbed a lot of extra building material, and time, and also increased the demand for heat because more external walls were exposed to the wind. . . . And at about the same time as coping with hundreds of sick and helpless adults the first births would be occurring, and babies would need frighteningly thorough care because the four infants who had been brought here had all died. . . .

We have means of neutralizing another of the native allergens, but the only way we can produce the compound on a scale large enough to be useful is by altering a diet-synthesizer. The changes will be irreversible with our limited equipment, but they will allow us to eat this land-plant, this seaweed, and this animal. Shall we do it? *No. We need our diet-synthesizers for the winter, when we can't get those things to eat.*

It's about Ornelle. She stole a stack of tubing from the main boiler and ran off saying she was going to make a spaceship so we can all go home. *So it's finally happened. Tell Jerode.*

Eighteen people down with acute diarrhea and a mild fever. Aykin, Fritch, Zanice, and Lodette are among them. We think it's analogous to amoeboid dysentery; it can be cured by the same drugs, but we have exactly five doses left. Jesset says it sounds like something that's endemic on the plateau, in which case we're due for a lot of it. Can we spare a diet-synthesizer long enough to produce a hundred doses for future use? *Yes, but be quick. We can't afford to let key people be ill.*

Sixty-five people have the sickness today. Same request. Fritch is better, so we're on course. *This time no. If it didn't kill people on the plateau it won't here. Put them on synthesizer cake and boiled water and see how long they take to recover of their own accord. Identify the infective organism and work out a way to neutralize it before it's swallowed.*

About the other refugees: couldn't we liberate them by—? *Sorry, Hosper. It won't work for this reason and that reason. It's no good moving before we're ready.*

The long term. *Always the dreadfully long term.*

How many pregnancies approved? I can't recall. Thirty-eight so far. *That's enough; close the register.*

How much more accommodation being laid out? Increase of thirty percent. *Not enough.* Shortage of timber. *Then find some clay upriver and float it down on rafts in ton lots; we'll make adobe kilns and bake some bricks. Use poured silica for the damp-course.*

Lodette, we're in rags. Linen used to be made from natural fibers prepared by rotting, pounding, sunning, etcetera. I want something like that.

Minty, here's a nice tough fiber. A spinning wheel works like this. A loom works like that.

Jesset, this is woven cloth. Some sort of garment that can be made up in a couple of hours, please.

Bendle, the sap of some trees can be spread on cloth and heat-treated to make it tough, resilient, and waterproof. We shall need shoes this winter.

Rothers, Jesset is going to make clothes. I want sewing needles and scissors. Here's a drawing.

Yes, Bendle? Oh. Well, how about the cortex of the trees? Animal-hide? Anything we can sew or mold or cut into usable footwear.

Yes, Jesset? Dyestuffs? Fine, but check for allergic reactions before a single garment is put on.

Yes, Minty? Oh, a waterwheel! Yes, why not? I'll draw you one. You could use an endless belt of your own thread to drive the loom.

No shortage of ideas, at least. . . .

Proposal: put a coffer-dam around the hull of the ship, pump out the water, cut up the metal with the thirty-five hundred degree beam of a solar furnace. *Might work, Aykin, but not this summer, I'm afraid.*

Proposal. hydroponics tanks in every living-house to supply fresh plant-food during the winter. *Good idea, but ask Bendle if we know enough about the needs of the native flora, Jerode if the diet supplement would repay the effort, Aldric if he can provide enough light to grow them. Three yeses or don't bother to come back.*

Proposal: sneak over the edge of the plateau by night and kidnap Gomes and his cronies. *Oh, stop bothering me.*

Proposal: blow up the other ship so Gomes no longer has an excuse to drive his workers. *You must be joking.*

Proposal: then you suggest a way to help those poor devils! *I promise. Yes, yes, I swear I will!*

Proposal: get out of that chair and come for a walk, because you'll make yourself ill if you don't take a break.

Lex leaned back and smiled up at Delvia. He said, "That's the best idea I've heard for at least three days."

Then he went on looking at her, thoughtfully. She had put on one of Jesset's rough but serviceable outfits consisting of a thigh-length tunic without sleeves, having big useful pockets made from a turn-up of the lower hem. In winter they would be combined with breeches buttoning at the ankle, and a coat. Most of the community had gladly replaced their original tattered clothing, though nothing was being thrown away that had any life in it.

Her hair was sun-bleached almost to whiteness, and she had the deep tan that all the outdoor workers had acquired. It had become known—there was no way of preventing it—that Lex was favoring her, and though people seemed a little puzzled, most were content to accept that they must have misjudged her. Life was much easier for her now, and she had lost her former air of continual tension.

He pushed back his chair and told the two women who were acting as his secretaries that he would be back in half an hour. Taking Delvia's arm, he walked out into the sunshine.

They turned toward the riverbank. When they had gone a hundred yards or so, he spoke meditatively.

"You're right; I am driving myself pretty hard. Know what the worst thing is?"

She shook her head.

"The sheer number of separate items. Soap, timber,

glue, nails, hammers, needles, spools for thread, cook-pots, spades and shovels, towels, blankets, bandages, boots. . . . I calculate that before the end of the summer we shall have to put more than a thousand things into production."

"So we can stay here in comfort," Delvia said.

"So we can stay here," he corrected. "Where none of us want to be." There was a pause. With a hasty shift of subject he went on, "By the way, has Naline talked to you? I hear she's—uh—very much calmer."

"Yes. She seems to have realized how stupid she was. I think she's going to grow up fast from now on, eventually turn out a nice person. I wish I could say the same about Ornelle. Is her case really hopeless?"

Lex gave a grim nod. "With our resources, the doc tells me. She takes everything she can lay hands on now and puts it on a pile, says she's going to make us a spaceship to go home in." He hesitated, and added in a lower tone, "I've never seen incurable insanity before. It isn't pretty."

"I imagine few people alive today have seen it," Delvia said. "But then, few people can realize how many individual things are involved in even a village society like ours. I certainly didn't. Lex, am I being very dumb, or is this a sensible question? I've been wondering over and over why we couldn't at least put an operating subradio into orbit. I'd have thought if we could do all this . . ." She gestured at the settlement they were leaving behind.

Lex thought for a moment. Then he said, "Do you have a watch?"

"Yes. But of course I'm not wearing it because—oh, you know! Nobody wears a watch now."

"Do you think a watch is as complicated as a subradio?"

"Of course not!"

"Even so, the timekeeping element of a modern watch is a crystal, machined to monomolecular tolerances, in a state of permanent resonance. In order to adjust it to the length of day we have here, we worked out that we'd need"—he began to count on his fingers—"ultrasonic cutting-tools, which we don't have; microscopes, which we don't have; a surface interferometer, which we don't have; a billimicron gauge, which we do have, but it's bent; a vacuum work-chamber; a radiation dust-sweep and gas-getter; a standard clock to calibrate it against; and about five years' observation to calibrate the standard.

Now to build the ultrasonic cutting-tool, you'd need—"

"All right, all right!" Smiling, Delvia put her hands over her ears. "But, look! We have the subradios—I mean we had, in the ship. Couldn't we have taken them out, and put them into orbit with a recording and a solar collector?"

"Yes, we just about could have," Lex said. "Aldric figured it out after we landed. Only not, unfortunately, in working order. His idea was to build a kind of gun out of the ship's disaster-box launcher; those shaped charges pack a lot of power, plenty to put a hundred pounds into orbit. The trouble was, the g-forces would smash flat anything we tried to fire."

"Then why didn't we leave the box in orbit before we came down?" Delvia pressed.

"Because we were worn out, half starved, and on the verge of suffocating," Lex snapped. "Forgotten?"

"Of course I haven't, but I'd have thought that you—"

"I tried," Lex said. "I was so ill and exhausted I had to give up. And if you tell anyone I tried and failed, I'll —never speak to you again."

The confession hung in the air like a cloud between them. They had come now to the riverside, and were standing looking inland toward the rapidly enlarging sedimentation plant. They could see Cheffy's team man-handling lengths of wooden pipe into position, and hear occasional shouted orders.

Suddenly there was a break in the rhythm of the work. One of the upriver guards—whom Lex had allowed himself almost to forget because he was already so obsessed with the plight of the other refugees—came running along the bank waving and shouting.

"People coming down the river! About a dozen of them! I saw a gun-beam! Stand to! Stand to!"

Lex drew a deep breath, all else instantly forgotten. So after all this time action was to be forced on him when he still was not ready. It wasn't likely that Gomes would have let runaways steal guns from him a second time. This must be the long-feared raid.

◈ XX ◈

He could scarcely recall how he had found the time to issue such detailed instructions, but he had done it, and they had been faithfully carried out. In addition to the camouflaged watchposts in the trees, from which the approaching party had just been spotted, he had ordered the preparation of what he thought of as a kind of trip-wire. A mile or so beyond the watchposts, but in plain sight of them, he had had more than twenty holes dug in the riverbank, so sited that it was hardly possible to avoid them; these holes had been covered with old black plastic, creased and torn so badly as to be useless for other purposes, to simulate the relaxed appearance of the bag-mouths of the underground carnivore.

Since Cardevant's party had found these to be so dangerous, Lex had reasoned that anyone else Gomes might send downriver would tend to panic on seeing such a cluster of the horrible objects. No matter how cautiously they had approached up to that point, they would be tempted to burn out what they took for a monster speci-men, and by the time they realized it was a dummy their gun-beams would have given them away.

The plan had worked to perfection. It did not depend on radio, which might have been overheard by the in-truders, or on a landline phone, for which they did not possess the spare cable, or on a line-of-sight beam phone which would have tied up precious lasers unproductively. As a result, he had been able to send Delvia running through the town calling the alarm when the party from the plateau were still out of earshot, and to reach the watchpost on the right bank of the river while they were still working out that they had been fooled.

Elbing was manning this watchpost; he had found his peg-leg more and more of a handicap, and was glad to volunteer for this chore and release someone else for work he could not do. As Lex scrambled up beside him into his

128

cage of boughs with the leaves still on, he gave a smile of greeting.

"They can't figure what hit them," he said. "Want a look?" He moved aside from the eyepiece of the ship telescope with which the post was equipped.

With a murmur of thanks Lex leaned toward it. The scope wasn't intended for such short-range work, and magnified so much that he could hardly get the whole of a man's height into view at once, but there was the distinct compensation that the newcomers' faces were as clear as they would have been at five paces.

"Gomes!' he exclaimed. "*And* Probian! Then maybe this isn't a raid after all. Maybe they've been driven to desperation and want a parley."

"I hope you're right," Elbing grunted. "Every last one of them has a gun, and we have two between eight hundred of us."

True enough, Lex noted. Now, Gomes's party was milling around on the opposite bank; Probian was angrily holding up a piece of charred plastic and swearing at the way they had been duped, while others poked sticks suspiciously into the pits as though unwilling to believe their eyes. It would obviously be several minutes before they moved on; he had the chance to study them at leisure.

There were eleven men altogether, he counted. An unusual number, with the interesting implication that only one gun had been left on the plateau. Who, incidentally, could Gomes have put in charge during his absence? After the defection of Hosper and Jesset it must have been hard for him to trust anybody. Was Cardevant with the party? Lex scrutinized each face in turn and found he wasn't. So it was probably him, though of course he might be dead, or too sick to travel.

"I had this kind of wild hope," Elbing ventured, "that they might have been driven out and come to beg for asylum. But that was before I saw they all had guns. What do you think, Lex?"

"Well, the likeliest explanation is that Gomes is finding his problems too much for him. But if things are really bad on the plateau, he'd be afraid that if he sent a deputy to the coast—even Probian—that might be the last he'd hear of him. He must be less worried about leaving his base than losing another of his handful of supporters."

"What could he need so badly that he has to come here in person, though?"

"Oh, it could be a lot of things—food, medical supplies, technical data. . . ." Lex shrugged.

"Think he's going to try to take what he wants at gunpoint?"

"Possibly. But if he has any sense at all, he'll more likely claim that he's in sight of getting his ship aloft, or maybe putting a subradio up at least, and wants aid to finish the job. He'll let the guns speak for themselves."

"You think he does have any sense, then? Way I hear it, he's pretty much out of his skull, isn't he?"

"If he were raving mad, then by this time one of his cronies would have ousted him. No, he must still be in possession of most of his faculties, maybe all of them apart from this obsession of his, and his streak of brutality." Lex sat back from the scope.

"Yes, I'm convinced he's on the verge of desperation. Everything points to it. Now I want the party to arrive in town in a bad state: nervy, on edge, as well as just tired and sick which they certainly must be. You have something to put the wind up them, don't you?"

Elbing grinned, pointing to a row of cords knotted around a branch within arm's reach. "We fixed about twenty or thirty of these in the bushes. I can make branches move at the corner of their eyes, that kind of thing. If they shoot, the cords will be cut and just snap back out of the way, so they won't find what caused the movement."

"Perfect. And we'll lay on a sort of show for them when they enter the town. I want them to get a first impression that'll kind of cow them. Try to hold them up as much as possible with your string-pulling, hm? It may take a while to get everybody organized."

He let himself over the edge of the watchpost floor and swarmed back to the ground.

Gomes and his companions came to the sedimentation plant and found it deserted. They spent a little while discussing it, giving nervous glances around them because for the past mile or more they had seen unaccountable movements in the undergrowth. They felt they were being watched. In fact they were. Cheffy's workers had been told to hide nearby and keep an eye on them.

Continuing, they came in sight of the town: solid-looking buildings of timber caulked with clay, their wooden-shuttered windows open to the hot summer air;

smoke rising from the chimneys of the brick kilns; a clangor of nailing, sawing, and chopping. They saw where timber had been felled, ground cleared, and replanted with salad-trees in neat tidy lines. They saw people healthy, well-nourished, in clean serviceable clothing, and were reminded that they were ragged, filthy, lean as scarecrows.

The people took notice of them—just a little. They did not interrupt what they were doing, which included the distribution of large bowls of savory-smelling food to workers on the job and the issuing of water rations from big barrels.

They stood overlooking the town for some minutes, uncertain what to do. Then Cheffy's men rose into sight from the nearby scrub, and with an oath the intruders whirled, covering them with their guns.

None of Cheffy's men was armed. Lex had specifically enjoined them not to take the guns from the watchposts. Yet.

Cheffy himself, approaching Gomes, said in a level voice, "We've been expecting you. Come along—I'll take you to our polymath."

"*What?*" The word ripped from Gomes's mouth as though it would tear his lips. "You have a polymath here? I don't believe it! Nobody said—"

"Captain," Probian said under his breath, putting a hand on Gomes's arm. He pointed at the thriving little town, and had no need to continue.

Reading the confusion on Gomes's rough-bearded face, Cheffy spoke again. "You may keep your guns, of course. I was told you'd feel insecure without them. But you won't have any cause to use them. This way, please."

He didn't pause to see their reaction, but turned and began to walk downslope. His gang moved behind him, encircling Gomes's party in such a fashion as to suggest they were escorting a group of extraordinary animals, making a parade of it. People working on the newly-erected houses here at the edge of town reinforced the impression as they improvised in accordance with Lex's order: "Make them feel like the barbarians they are!"

"Hi, Cheffy!" called Zanice, collecting bars of white soap from their setting-trays. "Pretty sorry lot they look, don't they?"

"Dirty!" Cheffy agreed. Gomes set his jaw and his grip on his gun tightened.

"Are those they?" Minty inquired, wrinkling her nose

as she sat on the step outside the single women's house, ladling hot soup out for members of Fritch's building team who were putting up new partitions inside. "Look as though they could use a good meal—and a bath!"

One of Gomes's companions swallowed so hard the noise was like a shout, and Probian rounded on him, his face thunderous.

It went on like that all the way to the headquarters hut —personal remarks being passed, never addressed to the strangers but simply commenting on their dirt, their stink, their raggedness and scrawniness—while Cheffy's gang watched like hawks for any sign that Gomes's temper was going to break.

It held. Just. As Lex had hoped, by the time the new arrivals were herded into a cluster in front of the headquarters hut, they were not only angry. They were also overwhelmed.

From here they could glimpse the installations down on the beach—stills, boilers, the solar furnace, and so on— and get the full measure of what had been accomplished here while they were crazily striving to repair their ship.

Lex let them stand in the sun for a minute. Then he pushed aside the curtain covering the doorway and emerged on the verandah.

"You?" Gomes said faintly. His voice shook. "You're a polymath?"

"In training," Lex said, looking the captain over. The first glance showed him something he hadn't spotted through the telescope. The twelfth gun was tucked in the top of Gomes's backpack, improvised out of a spacesuit and roughly tied with cord. So either they had simply deserted their base, or they'd devised some other weapon to keep the slaves cowed during their absence. Interesting!

He went on, "Well, what do you want? Apart, of course, from a bath with strong soap and a change of clothes." He sniffed exaggeratedly.

Gomes stifled an oath. He said angrily, "What the hell was the idea of digging those pits by the river?"

"What? Oh, those! They're to scare off animals that try to raid our orchards, of course. All the big herbivores are afraid of those underground traps. You too? Was that what happened to the man you lost on the way here?"

Gomes scowled and was not going to answer. But one of his companions, a young man Lex remembered seeing with Cardevant when his party was ambushed at the dam, took a step forward and exclaimed incredulously, "How did you know?"

"Shut your mouth, Dockle!" Gomes flared. "I'll do the talking, hear me?"

Lex, an enigmatic look on his face to suggest that for all they could tell he might have engineered or at least observed the death of their twelfth man, watched narrowly. This was a delicate situation; he needed to undermine the confidence of Gomes's supporters in their leader—yet he dared not risk a gun being fired. Despite being low on charge, as he guessed they must be, they could take precious lives or at least destroy buildings.

"I won't shut up!" Dockle said hysterically. "These people have a polymath to help them, and look at them! Are they hungry, sick, filthy the way we are? Are they—?"

"I said shut up!" Gomes lifted his gun, his knuckles white around the butt.

"Gomes, your personal quarrels are no concern of ours," Lex said quietly. "If you want to say something, go ahead. But be quick—I'm busy."

"You bastard!" Gomes blurted. "If only I'd known when I had you up on the plateau!"

"Known what I am, you mean? Why should I have told you? Would you expect me to help you with your futile project, aid and abet your brutal treatment of your slaves? No, I decided I'd simply wait until you got into the mess you're in now. Up on the plateau, you're no longer in control. People are demanding who's going to be alive for the rescuers to find even if you do put a subradio aloft. They're collapsing at work through fatigue, deficiency diseases, infections they have no resistance to. You've come here to beg for help—food, drugs, blankets, anything—because you're afraid you may wake up tomorrow and find your throat cut."

Every word printed more clearly on Gomes's face the accuracy of Lex's analysis. As he had requested, people had come drifting in to surround Gomes's party now, and they heard and saw for themselves. One more thing to cement his authority; he dared neglect no chance to reinforce it.

Gomes shouted, "I captained that ship! I know it can be repaired!"

"I say it can't," Lex contradicted coolly.

"You're not a spaceman! You don't know—"

"In polymath training one learns a lot of things," Lex

said, his voice like a knife. "Now listen to me. Your proposition is unacceptable to us. It's your turn to consider ours. We are extremely anxious to help our fellow castaways"—Arbogast, he recalled, had used that very phrase—"but our resources are limited and our survival is at stake. We will provide food, clothing, accommodation, whatever else is necessary, for everyone who survives on the plateau. To purchase it, you will lay down your guns now. And you, Gomes, you, Probian, and probably certain others—no doubt there will be a hundred witnesses to give the names—will be formally tried for crimes under the Unified Galactic Code; to wit murder, employment of slave labor, violence against the person, cruel and unusual punishment, and usurpation of unlawful authority. Well?"

"You devil!" Gomes said, almost in a whisper. "You—!" He raised his gun slowly until it was leveled at Lex's chest, and a murmur of dismay went through the watching crowd.

"These are *my* terms," he said. "Either you give us what we want, or I'll kill every last mother's son of you and burn your pretty little town for a funeral pyre. We've got guns. Twelve of them. You have only two. Come on, move!"

◇ XXI ◇

For the rest of his life Lex was to look back on that moment and recognize it as the turning point when his knowledge about himself converted into knowledge *of* himself. They had pressed him from every side to act against Gomes, to liberate the other refugees, to head an avenging army or a party of kidnappers. In fact, only some twenty days had elapsed since his return from the plateau, yet they had felt like an eternity because people had come to him a hundred times with schemes for action. He turned them down, showing the flaws in them if he had time, merely uttering a curt negative if he was busy. He had felt obscurely guilty, knowing that every day's delay might mean that another life or lives had been lost to Gomes's cruelty—but to go against madmen with plenty of energy guns would be suicide for some, at least, of the attackers.

Now, all of a sudden, he realized he had been right to hold back not only for that, but for another—far subtler—reason.

His decision could influence the whole future of humanity on this planet.

He was not afraid for his own life, even with Gomes's gun pointed at him. Polymath training had endowed him with reactions that no sick, half-starved old man could match. In the tenth of a second between Gomes closing his finger on the trigger and the lancing forth of the beam he could throw himself to one side, then spring at the captain, wrest the gun away, and have him at his mercy before any of his companions could respond.

But the object of polymath training wasn't to save his life.

He had been able to give directions for scores of projects which would eventually turn this handful of castaways into a flourishing society. But that wasn't the object of his training, either. He had assumed without question that it was.

How, though, was a man fitted to take charge of a brand-new planet? What faculty entitled him to shoulder such responsibility? Not quick reactions or superior physique or encyclopedic knowledge. Anyone could have any of the three, and as for the last there were libraries, computer stores, recording banks which could hold infinitely more data than any human brain.

No. The required talent was the ability to be right.

Given the sum of two plus x, the ordinary man said the question was unanswerable. The polymath was the man who answered it. Correctly.

Given a totally unexplored planet and a damaged spaceship, the polymath said, "Tame the planet." The ordinary man said, "Mend the ship." The planet was tameable; the ship was beyond repair.

Given strong personalities in conflict, endangering the safety of the refugees, the polymath said, "This one is valuable; that one is a handicap." The ordinary man said, "Well, there's a lot to be said on both sides. . . ." The valuable one worked like a fury; the other went insane and became a burden on the community.

Lex had had a mere fraction of the full polymath training and only the first stages of the physical modifications. But those had sufficed. The demands of the situation itself had completed the training well enough to crystallize the indispensable talent—that, and confrontation with the evidence of what could happen if the man in charge decided wrongly.

So also: given a lunatic dominating four hundred others at gunpoint, the ordinary man said, "We must liberate the persecuted, even if some of us are killed, even if many of them are killed." The polymath said, "A man who can be that wrong will hang himself."

And here was the man who could be that wrong, driven by the consequences of his actions to put his neck in the noose.

Very slowly, Lex smiled.

At first the others thought he was crazy to tell Gomes he could have all he wanted. Then they thought he was stalling for time, so that tiredness and greed would eventually distract the intruders and they could be overpowered when their minds were not on their guns. Then, as they discovered that neither of these explanations fitted, they began to wonder if he was frightened.

They obeyed his instructions—but they began to wonder.

The fearfulness that Gomes and his companions displayed was pitiable. They could not refuse the luxury of a hot bath, with soap of which there had been none on the plateau for months. But they refused to enter the bath-huts; they said that they wanted the water brought outside and poured into tubs where they could guard each other, guns at the ready.

Lex told his people to do as they were asked.

They could not refuse the offer of a square meal, but they would not let the food be brought to them ready prepared; they went in a suspicious group to the kitchen, inspected the diet-synthesizers to make sure the settings had not been tampered with, and when one of Bendle's students sprinkled antallergen on a salad of native greenstuff compelled her to sample it first and prove she hadn't poisoned it.

They could not refuse the offer of vitamin shots to help clear up the skin infections with which they all were afflicted; the sight of them stripped for the bath had been revolting, because they were patched with sores and scabs. Moreover, Gomes's swollen legs had become far worse thanks to his journey through the dense summer undergrowth along the river. But there too suspicion led them to insist that Jerode give himself an injection first.

Going with them from one place to another, Lex did not dare let a hint of his jubilation show on his face. He was worried that people might completely fail to understand his intentions, but it seemed that he had created enough trust in the community for no one to challenge him openly.

Your clothing is past hope: see if this will fit. . . . It does? Take it!

Your bedrolls are torn and filthy: we've made blankets now. Have some!

Your journey back will be tough: we have food to spare. Here you are!

Back at the headquarters hut, Gomes looked with satisfaction on everything they had been given. He still had his gun in his hand; now, glancing up at Lex, he gestured with it.

"Guess I should have brought more men, so's we could carry more stuff away!" he gibed. "Still, it looks like a gun talks about as loud as ten men on the average, and more with luck."

He spat in the dust. "So you're a polymath," he added. "But you can be just as dead as anybody else. So we're level."

Lex was very conscious of the many, many eyes turned on him. Everyone had left work to come and witness the appalling spectacle of Gomes and his men being loaded with as much as they could carry of the community's goods. To his regret and alarm, their thinking had apparently stopped there—even Jerode, Fritch, Aldric, Cheffy, did not seem to have asked themselves whether this single load of booty was a real prize for Gomes.

But he was not at all surprised to see that Delvia, standing in shade alongside the hut, was smiling to herself when none of Gomes's men were looking her way.

"Two more things," Gomes said. "Just a couple more. Lex, you still have a brace of energy guns. The way things are I believe they'd be more use to us than you. Get 'em!"

"No! No, you mustn't!"

From the front row of the audience Hosper ran out, to

confront Gomes with his face pale, his hands clenched.

"You!" Gomes said. "After what you did, I ought to use this gun on you!" His lip curled. "But why should I waste good charge?"

And he reversed the gun and swung it butt-first against Hosper's jaw.

A cry, and Jesset was trying to rush after her man, fingers like claws; if she had reached Gomes, she would have torn out his eyes. But someone was there to catch her, hold her, soothe her back to calmness.

Delvia.

If anyone tried to grade the community on a basis of potential for survival, Lex thought, Delvia would come a very good second to himself.

Gomes glared at Hosper, sprawled on the ground before him, then at Jesset panting while Delvia clutched her arm. He said, "Give me those guns, or I'll burn these two!"

"Go ahead!" Jesset shouted. "It's a cleaner death than what you're doing to the people on the plateau!"

"Who has the guns?" Lex said quietly. "Aldric, is it you? Let him have them."

"Thank you," Gomes said with immense sarcasm, wiping sweat from his face. "You talked pretty big at first, Mr. Polymath! But these guns talk bigger, don't they?"

Silently, with one glance at Lex as though he thought the community had been betrayed, Aldric placed the guns on top of one of the packs made up for Gomes's men.

"Right, that's almost all," Gomes said. "Now I want to make one thing clear. Don't follow us. Don't try to get up to the plateau. We have all the guns now, and we can spare the time to watch for you creeping up on us. Now I've seen how much you have down here, I can see it's going to be worthwhile coming back. So we will be back, guns and all, and we'll collect what we want when we want. Next time maybe we'll ask for more. And when we get our ship into orbit, we may be kind enough to mention that there are some other refugees here on this miserable mudball. Depends how well you behave, understand?"

He chuckled. At that moment Hosper, recovered from his blow on the jaw, made to gather himself and dive for Gomes's swollen legs. Probian moved quicker. His foot shot out, and Hosper went sprawling again, clutching his face and moaning.

"Thanks, Probian," Gomes acknowledged with a nod.

"I see I beat a spark of guts into Hosper, at any rate, even if the rest of you are only worried about your comfort and the whole skins you're so fond of."

He turned to his companions. "All right, load up. Let's get away from here before dark."

They moved obediently to shrug into their packs—all of them except Dockle. He was barely more than a boy, his face tanned to a burned-wood color, his limbs stalk-thin, his body meager. He stood rock-still, his blazing eyes on Gomes.

"That means you, Dockle," the captain rumbled.

"I'm not going," the boy said. "I'm not crazy."

There was a sudden icy hush across the heat of the day. All eyes—Gomes's, his companions', the watchers'—turned to Dockle.

"I'm not going!" he repeated more loudly, and his voice was ragged at the edge of barely-suppressed tears. "I don't want to go back to that hell of yours! You'll never fix the ship! We've slaved over it for months, and all we've done is lift it up and show how badly the belly's smashed. If we work the rest of the summer we'll never get it ready, and if we don't prepare for the winter we'll all die of cold. I'm not going back!"

A wave of anger could be felt passing through the crowd. Lex knew it was directed at him. How could he stop a suicidal attack on Gomes's party after what Dockle had said? Even now he was sure no one else had followed his reasoning. Yet what he had in mind felt *right*. It didn't feel as though it would lead to the horror of eight hundred people without weapons being massacred by eleven with energy guns.

And then, when he had begun to doubt his talent for being right within an hour or two of discovering it, Gomes provided him with the missing answer.

"Pick up that pack, Dockle," he said in a low, threatening voice. "Because life down here isn't going to be so pleasant after today. Sure it's tough to get a ship fixed without proper facilities. But a polymath is claimed to be a substitute for just about everything."

He whipped around, and his gun was once more leveled at Lex.

"You! Get down here! You're a valuable property, and we don't intend to leave you behind!"

The wave that passed through the crowd this time was of indrawn breaths, a collective gasp of dismay. Lex let it die. He wanted everyone who was watching—except Gomes and his men—to see with clear eyes the precise manner of his obedience.

He said, "Very well. If that's what you really want. But I won't answer for the consequences."

"Then I won't answer for your survival!" Gomes snapped. "There'll be two men watching you all the time with guns, so you'll do as you're told. There aren't any more like Hosper on the plateau. We cleaned house." He cast a glance at Dockle and jerked his head. Reluctantly, but now unable to keep his defiance up, the boy gathered his pack and strapped it on.

Probian had a rope. While the others held back the crowd with their guns he fixed it around Lex's wrists, lashing them securely behind his back and taking the slack as a kind of leash.

"Move," Gomes said curtly, and added with raised voice, "Anything you do to try to stop us, your boy Lex is the first to suffer. Keep your distance, all of you!"

◆ XXII ◆

Helpless, the crowd followed to the edge of town, hoping for some sign or clue from Lex which they would have obeyed in spite of the threatening guns. But Lex walked steadily among his captors, not looking back.

Clenching his fists in impotent fury as he watched the thieves dwindle along the riverbank, Fritch burst out, "What came over him? We'll never get him away from them now! He must be out of his mind!"

"He knows what he's doing!" Delvia flared, rounding on him.

"How can you be so sure?" Fritch snapped.

"He's a polymath, isn't he?"

"Polymath or not, he's only young. And he's only had part of the training."

"Right," Rothers said from a few yards away. "What's

more, he turned out to be too fond of life to stand up against a gun."

"I think you're wrong," Cheffy countered. Now they were gathering into tight groups as the argument broke into a dozen angry shifting fragments. "He's seen for himself what conditions are like on the plateau. You've heard Hosper, Jesset, the others—you know it would be better to die than fall into Gomes's hands, and so does he. He must have something figured out!"

From somewhere at the back of the crowd, Nanseltine shouldered his way toward them. Not much had been heard of him since his deflation at the assembly where Lex assumed command, but from his manner now it was clear he'd seen a chance to revert to his old blustering.

"Sure, he may well have figured something out!" he exclaimed. "Nothing that will help us, though! What if Gomes does manage to refit his ship with Lex's help? Next thing you know, we'll see it taking off with him and Gomes on board—"

The words exploded into a cry; and Nanseltine drew back, his hand to his reddening cheek. Panting, Delvia stood before him, arm raised for a second blow.

"Just because that's exactly what you'd like to do, don't accuse Lex of it, damn you! And the rest of you!" She whirled on the committee members surrounding her. "You're practically as bad, laying all the responsibility on Lex and then panicking when he does something cleverer than you could have thought of!"

There was a momentary silence. Aldric appealed to Jerode. "Doc, you think she could be right?"

"I don't know." Jerode passed his hand over his bald scalp. "I must say I find it very hard to believe Lex would give in meekly without some purpose behind it. But it seems like a desperate gamble in any case, and frankly I haven't the least notion what he has in mind."

"I can see one good reason for him to act as he did," Delvia said. "Suppose we'd tried to overpower Gomes's men. They'd have killed fifty of us easily and some of them would probably have got away. They'd have smashed our equipment, set fire to the buildings—we'd be in a hell of a mess! Lex cares about what happens to us; don't you know that? And he cares just as much about the others on the plateau! You don't believe that? Just because he kept turning down harebrained schemes that wouldn't have freed them?"

She had the whole attention of the crowd now. Eyes blazing, voice ringing, she stormed on.

"Gomes said he'd cleaned house up there, got rid of traitors! But you heard what Dockle said, didn't you, right to Gomes's face? If his people hate Gomes that much, what's going to happen when he gets back with his loot? Is he going to share it around among everybody? Hm? They're going to hate him worse than ever. And with Lex right there among them—well!"

"But just one man against so many," Fritch worried.

"Lex isn't an ordinary man," Delvia insisted. "Baffin, didn't he lead you back, eight people and one of you injured, in the dark with Gomes's men after you?"

"That's so," Baffin agreed. "He said he can see in the dark."

"He told me that too," Jerode said. "It's one of his polymath modifications."

"Well, then!" Delvia appealed to the crowd. "Gomes hasn't got you or me to cope with. He's got a ticking bomb! My guess is that Lex will be running things on the plateau his own way inside the week."

"You make out a good case for your wonder-boy, Delvia," Fritch grunted. "But like Gomes said, he's a valuable property. We can't just leave him to manage by himself."

"I say we can and should," Delvia snapped.

Jerode pondered for a moment. Finally he drew himself up. "I'm afraid Fritch is right," he said. "We'll have to send a party after him. What they can do without weapons, I don't know, but—oh, perhaps they could ambush Gomes's men while they're asleep. At the very least we must know what's happening. Baffin, you've done the trip more often than the rest. Pick your men."

Hosper, his face discolored with angry bruises, strode forward at once, and Jesset came with him, clinging to his arm. Fritch stepped up also; then Aykin, Cheffy, Aldric, and others.

"Baffin, whatever you do, don't interfere!" Delvia pleaded. He shrugged and didn't answer.

It took some time to organize handlights, hatchets, rations, and other necessities, and it was late in the afternoon before the party was ready to move off. Baffin set a rapid pace. They passed the watchposts, then the site of Lex's ingenious trap which had caused Gomes's men to reveal themselves.

A short distance past that point, Baffin gave a cry and pointed ahead.

"What is it?" Fritch demanded.

"I saw a gun-beam," Baffin muttered. "Quicker! Come on!"

Mouths dry with apprehension, hearts pounding and lungs straining as they strove to keep up, they followed him through the whipping undergrowth. They had gone another mile and a half when they found the body.

Two thin legs protruded from a bush heavy with mid-summer foliage; the feet were bare. Insectoids were coming to explore the flesh, crawling out of the bush and up from the ground.

Horrified, they halted. Baffin tugged aside the concealing stems and they recognized the corpse.

"It's the youngster," Fritch said, swallowing hard.

A bolt had seared Dockle from throat to waist. He had been stripped of everything he possessed except the charred shirt clinging to his ruined flesh. Out of his scream-open mouth the native carrion-takers were already running.

"Don't stand around!" Hosper said with violence. "Let's get after them—it'll be Lex next!"

But Baffin was staring down at the body, his face set in a meditative frown. "I . . . wonder," he said at last. "You know, somehow I don't think so. I'm beginning to see what Delvia meant."

The trouble started sooner than Lex had dared to hope. As soon as they were out of sight of the town, Gomes's party split into two clearly-defined groups. Gomes, with Probian and most of the others, went at the front, keeping Lex himself in the center with Probian holding his rope-leash. But Dockle and two others, the youngest of the party, kept a short distance behind, talking together in low voices.

More than once Gomes snarled at them to keep up. Yet Dockle in particular lagged, and at a point where the vegetation was exceptionally thick, he fell far enough back to be out of sight.

Twenty more paces, and Gomes caught on. He glanced back, discovered that Dockle had vanished, and gave an oath as he thrust past Lex, raising his gun. His heavy pack

caught overhanging branches and made them whine in
the air like whiplashes.

They did not see what happened, but they heard: Gomes
called Dockle a foul name and told him to come back;
there was a hysterical answer, and then came the flash
of the gun.

Gomes returned a moment later. "Get down there and
pick up his stuff," he said gruffly to the youngsters who
had been walking with Dockle. "Load it on Lex's back.
And take a good look at Dockle while you're about it,
because that's what will happen to you if you try the same
trick."

The two looked as though they were going to vomit,
but they obeyed.

One down, ten to go. Another before dark would be
advisable, Lex calculated coldly. He would have preferred
that Dockle should live, because he had had the guts to
defy Gomes not once but twice, but he knew enough about
the situation on the plateau to imagine what Dockle must
have done or connived at for Gomes to choose him as a
companion. He wasn't thinking of justice or retribution,
though. What counted was the future of humanity on this
planet.

No one said anything for a long time after that; they
just plodded onward. The going was better than it had
been on his last trip. On the way down Gomes had had
a lot of foliage burned back, and it had not grown over
the path yet, though it was so luxuriant it would restore
itself in another week.

An hour from town they passed the dead remains of
one of the black-bag monsters, presumably the one which
had killed a man on the party's coastward journey. They
were astonishingly numerous. Something would eventually have to be done to protect humans from them, though
they could not be eliminated—their ecological function,
obviously, was to prevent herbivores overgrazing the
plants. The next patch of them was only a half-mile farther on. Lex's ultra-keen hearing identified a bubbling
noise in the river well before anyone else did, and he
watched closely to see if his captors knew what such a
sound signified. Apparently they didn't. Nor did they recognize the blue-green shoots on the unbrowsed trees
nearby. On the way down they must have contrived to
avoid this particular carnivore, despite its being con-
cealed by the pseudo-moss which here spread densely on

the ground. Perhaps at that time it had just fed and wasn't interested in further prey. But now . . .?

Not Gomes. Not Probian. Without seeming to change his direction Lex stepped adroitly among the bag-mouths, and because they were in a line with him Gomes and Probian also escaped. But the man next behind was walking slightly to one side, and his left leg suddenly plunged downward.

At once there were screams, and guns flared. It was altogether convincing that Lex should leap aside in terror like everyone else, and jerk Probian with the rope so that his beam burned not into the ghastly black maw but into the legs and belly of the captive.

By the time darkness overtook them, Gomes's party was in a very bad state. They cleared a large patch with their guns, then built a big fire, not for warmth but for comfort, since the night was hot.

Probian, glowering, hobbled Lex with the rest of the rope and left his arms bound behind him. He was given no food, though a grudging mouthful of water was accorded him. The others ate, not talking, but looking about them fearfully at intervals. They avoided meeting Gomes's eyes.

Good.

Gomes set up a rota to keep watch on Lex. Two wakeful men with guns were to be facing him continuously until dawn. He did not include himself in the rota. He made sure that the two young men who had been walking with Dockle were not going to watch together. They knew why, and so did everyone else. Also good. The more hints about deserting Gomes that crossed their minds, the better.

He noted carefully which of his guards-to-be went into the undergrowth before turning in, to relieve themselves. One didn't, but drank greedily from his canteen before throwing himself, exhausted, on his bedroll.

Perfect. That was the man Gomes had assigned to watch with Probian after midnight. Lex leaned back and dozed.

As he had figured, the first pair of guards were too eager to lie down to permit the man he was counting on to relieve himself before assuming his duty. They made him turn out and take his place at once. Growing more uncomfortable by the minute, he sat with gun in hand until the others were snoring. Lex feigned deep sleep.

At last the man's bladder could endure it no longer. He spoke to Probian, handed over his gun, and d'sappeared out of the circle of light from the low-burning fire.

Under cover of the darkness Lex had been quietly fraying his bonds. Now he snapped them at wrists and feet and hurled himself at Probian. The man did not even have time to cry out before his head jolted back. After that he was unconscious.

Moral, thought Lex as he stole after the second guard to catch him from behind: an ordinary rope could not hold a polymath for long.

Though it served admirably as a garrote.

He had made no more sound than a passing breeze, and the others were too exhausted to be easily woken. They remained slumped on their bedrolls as he stole from one to the next collecting all their guns except Gomes's and stringing them together on his rope.

Then, ghostly, he faded into the dark. At the very edge of hearing he could detect noises from downriver. Presumably Jerode or someone had sent "rescuers" after him. He must intercept them before they came so close that they disturbed Gomes's gang.

◈ XXIII ◈

By the time they found the second body, partly burned, partly digested by the crippled bag-monster, Baffin's team was prepared to accept that Delvia had been right. They couldn't imagine how it was being done, but they realized Lex must be trying to demoralize his captors to the point at which Gomes would lose control.

They saw, as night was falling, how guns were being used to clear a campsite ahead. Then a fire was lit, and the flames reflected on the nearby trees. Baffin decided not to do the same, but with great caution to follow the trail in the dark in the hope of mounting a sneak attack.

It was while they were stealing through the night that Lex appeared in front of them, grinning broadly and holding up his strung-together guns like a successful fisherman.

They were so taken aback that at first they could not react. Fritch broke the tension with a mutter of sincere— if reluctant——admiration.

"You young devil! How did you manage it?"

Lex explained briefly, distributing the guns as he talked. There were almost enough to go around.

"You didn't get them all!" Baffin said, having counted.

"No, I left one with Gomes," Lex agreed. "For a reason, don't worry. Now listen carefully to me. All hell is due to break loose, and we'll have to pick up the pieces. I want some of you to come with me—Hosper, you and Jesset because you know the layout on the plateau, and you, Aldric, and you, Cheffy. Baffin, I want the rest of you to camp down here. About dawn they'll find out what's happened. Gomes may finish them because he'll be so furious, but some of them will probably get away and come back downriver. Wait for them; when they get here, take them to the town under guard. Then tell Jerode to make up a big relief party, with all his nurses who aren't pregnant. Bring blankets, clothes, food, anything you can. By the time that stuff can be brought to the plateau, it's going to be desperately needed. Plan for at least two hundred sick and injured, and everyone weak and exhausted."

He gave a faint chuckle.

"Gomes's situation must have been disastrous enough when he set out for the coast. You figure what will happen when he gets back having lost all but one gun, and probably all but one companion."

There were answering smiles.

He beckoned to the four he had detailed to go with him, turning as he spoke.

"Follow me. Move quietly. We're going back to watch what happens when Gomes wakes up."

Gomes rolled over, grunting, blinked his eyes open. One second later he was sitting up, hand on his gun, and shouting at the top of his voice. It was barely dawn; the light was watery-gray. Probian lay sprawled on the ground, breathing stertorously. There was no sign of his fellow-guard, and the other six men were sleeping soundly. The prisoner, of course, was gone.

From the safety of two hundred yards away, high in

a tree, Lex's keen vision could plainly discern what was
happening. There had been almost total silence for an
hour past, and his hearing was fined to such keenness
that he could clearly hear the quarrel mounting. The par-
ticipants made it easy by bellowing at each other. Gomes
was practically out of his mind with fury; at first he
screamed that the missing man was a traitor like Dockle,
then, when he was found in the undergrowth, that he
and Probian were incompetent fools.

They roused Probian by throwing water over him, and
he was so dazed that he could give no account of what
had happened. His incoherence roused Gomes to explosion point. He made to kick Probian in the face. One of
the other men jumped him from behind, demanding
whether they were all to be treated as animals now.

His companions shared his view. Mouthing hysterically, Gomes threatened them with his gun, calling them
defeatists who had sold out to the people at the coast.
The men exchanged frightened glances. One of them
moved to Gomes's side—most likely, persuaded by the
gun.

Now Gomes tried to compel them to go back downriver and recapture Lex, claiming he couldn't have gone
far. Lex smiled to himself. Quite right. But that order
was the last straw on the men's backs.

They spread out as though to comply, collecting their
belongings; then one of them, passing by the dying fire,
snatched up a brand from it and threw it at the captain.
At the end of its charge, his gun only flashed, no more
than singeing his attacker. The rest piled on him and
brought him down.

There was a brief conference. All the heart had gone
out of them. They were sick and tired of slaving for
Gomes, even those who up to now had most faithfully
carried out his orders. Down at the coast there was a
polymath, and if he could get away with two armed men
guarding him and seven others sleeping nearby, there was
no limit to what he might ultimately achieve.

They left Gomes, and Probian, and the man Lex had
strangled, and took the empty gun, no doubt for purposes of bluff. Then, in a strung-out line, they headed
back downriver.

. Perfect.

Those six deserters had long been captured by Baffin's
party and escorted to the town, when Gomes began to

recover. The day was bright and hot. He climbed dizzily to his feet, found himself with only two companions now, and cursed the men who had abandoned him. He staggered to the river and sluiced himself with water, then roused Probian, who lay in a near-coma.

With kicks and oaths he drove the others to their feet, made them pick up what little gear the deserters had left them, and urged them onward, upriver.

Discreetly, occasionally coming close enough to see them but following mostly by sound, Lex led his team after them.

The man who had been strangled collapsed late in the afternoon, and not all Gomes's screams and insults could make him continue. Gomes and Probian abandoned him, and Lex assigned Aldric to make him comfortable, provide him with food and water, and tell him that he would be rescued when the main relief party came by. That of course would not be before tomorrow.

The vegetation closed tunnelwise around the river. Sustained now by sheer desperation, Gomes and Probian plodded on, always with Lex's party a few hundred yards behind. Night came down, and they reached a site previously cleared, where they slumped down, so exhausted they could barely snatch a mouthful of food and water. Now the torture to which they were submitting the pair began to trouble Lex's companions; even Jesset, who had at first said hotly that nothing was too bad for such devils, fell silent when she saw the state to which they were reduced.

His eyes like chips of rock, Lex stared up toward the cleared ground where the hapless men lay sleeping. He said, "If we wake them a little after midnight, we can reach the plateau at first light tomorrow. Get a few hours' sleep. You're going to need it, I promise."

In the dead heart of the night they crept up on Gomes and Probian and woke them with handlights in their eyes. They were too weary to offer resistance. Fed, given water, they were taken captive in their turn, and driven onward again. Soon they were on high ground, having to clamber over the rocky ledges beside the falls and rapids, with starlight and Lex to show the way. Sometimes having to drag the prisoners, or lift them over the worst obstacles, they nonetheless made good time. Dawn was just breaking as they found themselves below the sad, futile remains of

Gomes's vaunted dam. The river ran free now, and its
sound was loud enough to cover a few quietly-spoken
words.

"I'm going up first," Lex whispered. "Send Gomes and
Probian after me, then follow yourselves, as quickly as
you can."

The others nodded. Gleefully Hosper hugged Jesset to
him with his left arm, weighing his gun in his other hand.

"And don't use that unless you have to," Lex ordered.

He scrambled over the last rocky shelf, and was on
the same level as the wrecked dam. He had judged that
the gap here would be guarded, and he was right. As he
turned and dragged the unprotesting Gomes up behind
him, he heard a hiss of breath, and then someone said
sharply, "Say, it looks like the captain got back!"

A handlight beam, very faint in the morning twilight,
slanted down and fell on Gomes and Probian standing
dazed on the edge of the rock-shelf. After a moment two
men emerged from cover, carrying—for want of energy
guns—crossbows improvised from springy strips of metal
and fraying lengths of cord.

That summed up everything which had gone amiss
here: that amount of ingenuity, lavished on arms. . . .

He waited a moment, judged it was safe to beckon the
others up beside him—and was wrong. Gomes licked his
lips.

"Get back!" he croaked. "It's a trap!"

Lex kicked his legs from under him, sent him sprawling. Probian made to run forward; Lex caught his arm,
spun him around, and dragged him to the ground. The
same movement avoided a metal-spiked quarrel from the
crossbow of the nearer guard.

Not as quiet and simple as he had been hoping. However, it could have been worse.

Half over the rock-shelf, Cheffy was sighting his gun
on the guards. Lex knocked it aside before he could fire.

"What's the idea?" he called angrily in a feigned voice,
relying on the half-darkness to keep the guards confused.
"The captain's gone out of his mind! He killed Dockle!
And we lost—oh, just come here and give me a hand!"

Bending, he whispered to Hosper and Jesset, "Stay out
of sight for a moment! Aldric, Cheffy, come up quickly
but keep your heads turned, don't let them see your faces!"

Bewildered, the guards—there were only the two of
them—came closer in response to the ring of authority

in Lex's tone. To prevent them recognizing him, he bent down over Gomes, muttering something about their trouble on the way.

And the moment the puzzled guards were near enough, he knocked them off balance.

Responding as though the job had been rehearsed, Aldric and Cheffy gave each of them the extra push necessary to send them over the lip of the rock, and as they fell Hosper and Jesset pounced to beat them into unconsciousness.

"Not so savage!" Lex snapped. "Remember, that's what we came to put a stop to!"

A little shamefacedly, they left their victims and climbed up to join the others. Expertly, Lex directed the tying-up of Gomes and Probian; when they were securely lashed they were carried into a shadowed dip between the ruined halves of the dam.

Under his breath Lex issued his next orders.

"Hosper, Jesset—you know the way around. One of you go with Aldric, one with Cheffy, and deal with the guard on the workers' pens. Don't shoot unless it's unavoidable. They may be alert because of the noise out here, but most of it will have been masked by the river splashing. Don't go near the ship—I'll see to that part. Then free as many of the workers as you can, immediately. I take it we can rely on all those who are kept chained, Hosper?"

The shock-headed man gave a bitter laugh. "After a while up here you forget there's such a word as 'trust'! But the only people who are on Gomes's side will be sleeping in the ship, probably barricaded in."

"OK," Lex said. "Carry on, then—and try not to make too much noise."

That was a pious hope. There was a period of about ten minutes when the gray light of early morning lay like a stifling blanket across the plateau, which Lex spent worming his way toward the hull of the ship. Some progress had been made in raising it; it lay now on four piles of rock, its underside clear of the ground, networked with cracks and splits. Just as he reached a spot from which he could cover its main access lock, there was a scream, and time began to run out.

A clanging alarm bell sounded. The lock flew wide. A terrific animal clamor rose from the workers' pens, and haggard men and women, their wrists and ankles galled with chains, began to pour like angry hornets across the plateau. In the lock's opening Cardevant appeared, and another man whom Lex recognized, one carrying another of the crossbows, both with whips. They stood irresolute for a second as they saw the freed workers boiling toward them like lava from a newly-erupted volcano, then took a unison pace forward as though determined to defy no matter what odds.

Lex sighted carefully and burned the whip out of Cardevant's hand. He gauged the power so accurately, there was barely a gleam on the hull at his back.

That was more than they could take. In terror they dived back into shelter and slammed the door behind them. Splendid. They could stew there as long as they liked.

Now, keeping one eye on the ship for any sign of another attempt to emerge, Lex rose into plain sight of the workers, tucking his gun into his belt as an indication of his peaceful intentions.

Shouting, he waved them to assemble around him. "We've come to rescue you! We're from the coast! You're free now! It's all over! We're bringing you food and medicine and clothes, and we have Gomes prisoner! You can stop being afraid!"

Wavering, bewildered, they swirled around him with vague eyes, some of them staring at their wrists as though they could not believe their fetters were actually gone. Not a few of them had started to weep.

He had just decided he could afford to relax, when there was a sound behind him which was the most frightening noise he would ever hear in his life, more fearful than the wind wailing across the locks of Arbogast's ship in the dead of last winter. It was the sound of fusion engines warming up.

In complete incredulity, to the accompaniment of screams from the workers, he turned. And saw the cracked hull of the starship rising slowly from the ground.

◆ XXIV ◆

The cosmos had suddenly become an insane place. full of giddy whirling lights. Yet somehow he was still master of himself and knew what had to be done. He ran forward, away from the ship, shouting at the top of his voice above the climaxing roar of the spacedrive.

"Lie down! Cover your eyes! Keep your mouths open!"

Conditioned by intolerable months of blind obedience, the workers heard him and did as he said, falling like wheat before a sickle. He ran on, catching sight of Hosper and Cheffy emerging from one of the stinking adobe sheds in the wake of the latest group they had freed. Appalled, Hosper was about to fire on the ship.

"Hosper! *Don't!*" Lex yelled. And Cheffy, responding, caught his companion's arm.

"You can't let them go!" Hosper shrieked.

"Do you think they can?" Lex bawled back. *"Get down!"* He flung himself forward on the stony ground and opened his mouth wide as the terrible noise beat at his ears. His whole field of vision embraced only the pebbles and dirt under his face. The noise went on.

Were they going to make it? By some crazy miracle, were they? He felt sweat crawl down his face and his palms were sticky. Let them do it! Let them get into orbit, let Gomes be proved right and Lex be wrong, let him have condemned his fellows needlessly to being stranded on a lonely planet when drive and determination could have sent out a call for help and brought rescuers faster than light. . . .

The landscape was lit with unbearable brilliance now, and every grain of sand under Lex's face was etched sharp by shadow. He dared not look up.

The noise was fading. There was a wind. The angle of the tiny shadows was changing. He put his hands over his face and rolled on his side, risking a peep between his fingers. Shining like a new star, the ship was creeping into the sky. All around him he heard that other people were staring too, heedless of dazzling light. He identified a weeping voice as that of Jesset, and it mingled with the moans of a hundred others.

And then . . .

He pushed himself up on his knees and looked without shading his eyes. The ship was a mile high, two miles, dwindling and accelerating into the blue edge of the dawn. Silence was falling on the plateau, barely disturbed by a few final moans. They were all staring now, in awe, *willing* the ship to rise. With no reservation at all Lex wished like the rest.

A beacon of all their hopes, the light shrank into the sky. A smudge, a pinpoint. A dust-mote.

A . . . a pinpoint? A . . . a smudge? A smear!

Back down the blue field of the morning, out beyond the land where the reflection of the sun lay like a road of gold across the smooth summer sea, the ship returned. Lucifer cast from heaven, it tore the air asunder and rode the terrible light of its own destruction downward to the water—and was gone. Where it plunged, there came back a single monstrous bubble full of flames. A long time later the sea beat sluggishly against the beach.

His eyes still filled with the departed vision, Lex grew little by little aware that he was pounding the ground with his fists and that dry, formless sobs were racking his throat.

Later, when they asked to be told what to do about the miserable half-human wrecks of Gomes's tyranny, he refused an answer and went to sit by himself among the rocks, his head bowed.

"Lex! Lex!"

He stirred and looked up. Diffident, Delvia stood before him, her fair hair shaken back, a gun in her hand. There was a wealth of sadness in her eyes. He forced himself back to awareness, amazed that so much time should have passed, and gazed around the plateau, expecting to see the relief expedition at work. Instead, there were only a handful of newcomers, besieged by the desperate wretches he had liberated.

"Is that all Jerrode sent?" he demanded, jumping to his feet.

"No, no!" She caught his arm. "There are fifty of us coming altogether, with everything we can carry! But when we saw the ship go up a few of us thought we should hurry the rest of the way, in case things were out of control on the plateau. And . . ."

"What?"

"And I wanted to see you, Lex. I could imagine the way you must be feeling. Not the way Gomes planned, but in another five years, ten years, maybe we could have fixed the ship, or done something." Her words were pouring out in a rush, as though she had to get them all spoken before he could interrupt. "And those fools have thrown away that last tiny chance, and they've really finally and definitely burdened you with the troubles of a whole world, haven't they?"

Her lips trembled and her eyes grew large with tears. "But you're going to make it; I know you will. You're going to show us how to live here and we're going to have children and we're going to teach them all we know and we'll find ore and make tools and have farms and cities, and one day we're going to send a message back to tell people where we are, and they'll come and find us, they'll say you're the most wonderful man who ever lived because you realized we mustn't found our world's history on an army, on a war, on killing. . . ."

The words faded into a sob.

Lex stood rock-still for a moment; then he put his arm around her and gently kissed her hair.

"At least there's one person who understands," he murmured. "But you left out one thing that's perhaps more important than all the rest. You're right about the army, the war—but above all we had to be stopped from deluding ourselves with a false hope. That's worse than no hope at all."

He felt the terror which had gripped him for so long leak away. His voice was perfectly calm and level.

"You know something? I figured out when Gomes came to the town what it is that a polymath has to do. He has to be right. Always and without exception. Nothing else is good enough."

"What a terrible thing," she whispered.

"Yes, it is. And I was so afraid that I was wrong after all. . . . But at least now there's only one course open, so I can't choose wrong. Come along, Del. We've got to go and set our home in order." A shadow lingered on his face which belied his light tone.

Now, definitively, without trace of doubt or chance of

qualification: home. All they had. Where their children would be born, where they would be buried.

But it's going to be a good world eventually.

He hadn't meant to say the words aloud, and it was only when he saw Delvia smiling that he realized he had done so. Of course, saying it made it true. A polymath, after all, must always be right.

He took her arm and they walked forward together.

- ☐ **THE BOOK OF BRIAN ALDISS** by Brian W. Aldiss. A new and wonderful collection of his latest science fiction and fantasy masterpieces. (#UQ1029—95¢)

- ☐ **THE BOOK OF FRITZ LEIBER** by Fritz Leiber. A five-times Hugo winner selects his widest range of tales and articles. (#UQ1091—95¢)

- ☐ **THE BOOK OF PHILIP K. DICK** by Philip K. Dick. A new treasury of the author's most unusual science fiction. (#UQ1044—95¢)

- ☐ **THE BOOK OF FRANK HERBERT** by Frank Herbert. Ten mind-tingling tales by the author of DUNE. (#UQ1039—95¢)

- ☐ **THE BOOK OF VAN VOGT** by A. E. van Vogt. A brand new collection of original and never-before anthologized novelettes and tales by this leading SF writer. (#UQ1004—95¢)

- ☐ **STRANGE DOINGS** by R. A. Lafferty. Sixteen of the most astonishing stories ever written! (#UQ1050—95¢)

DAW BOOKS are represented by the publishers of Signet and Mentor Books, THE NEW AMERICAN LIBRARY, INC.

Presenting the international science fiction spectrum:

☐ **THE ORCHID CAGE by Herbert W. Franke.** The problem of robots and intelligence as confronted by Germany's master of hard-core science fiction. (#UQ1082—95¢)

☐ **GAMES PSYBORGS PLAY by Pierre Barbet.** They made a whole world their arena and a whole race their pawns. (#UQ1087—95¢)

☐ **WHERE WERE YOU LAST PLUTERDAY? by Paul Van Herck.** The winner of the Europa Award for the best sf novel from Belgium. You never read anything like it! (#UQ1051—95¢)

☐ **BAPHOMET'S METEOR by Pierre Barbet.** A startling counter-history of atomic Crusaders and an alternate world. (#UQ1035—95¢)

☐ **BERNHARD THE CONQUEROR by Sam J. Lundwall.** A tour-de-force by Sweden's science fiction expert—the novel of a 20,000-mile-long spaceship! (#UQ1058—95¢)

☐ **STARMASTERS' GAMBIT by Gerard Klein.** Games players of the cosmos—an interstellar adventure equal to the best. (#UQ1068—95¢)

DAW BOOKS are represented by the publishers of Signet and Mentor Books, THE NEW AMERICAN LIBRARY, INC.

DAW·sf BOOKS

- ☐ **THE CRYSTAL GRYPHON by Andre Norton.** The latest in the bestselling Witch World series, it is an outstanding other-world adventure.   (#UQ1076—95¢)

- ☐ **DARKOVER LANDFALL by Marion Zimmer Bradley.** No Earth-born tradition can withstand the Ghost Wind's gale.   (#UQ1036—95¢)

- ☐ **MAYENNE by E. C. Tubb.** Dumarest encounters a sentient planet in his long quest for the lost Earth.   (#UQ1054—95¢)

- ☐ **JONDELLE by E. C. Tubb.** Dumarest's trail to Lost Terra leads through a city of paranoid kidnappers.   (#UQ1075—95¢)

- ☐ **MIRROR IMAGE by Michael G. Coney.** They could be either your most beloved object or your living nightmare!   (#UQ1031—95¢)

- ☐ **FRIENDS COME IN BOXES by Michael G. Coney.** The problem of immortality confronts one deathless day in the 22nd Century.   (#UQ1056—95¢)

- ☐ **THE OTHER LOG OF PHILEAS FOGG by Philip José Farmer.** The interstellar secret behind those eighty days . . .   (#UQ1048—95¢)

DAW BOOKS are represented by the publishers of Signet and Mentor Books, THE NEW AMERICAN LIBRARY, INC.

THE NEW AMERICAN LIBRARY, INC.,
P.O. Box 999, Bergenfield, New Jersey 07621

Please send me the DAW BOOKS I have checked above. I am enclosing
$_____(check or money order—no currency or C.O.D.'s).
Please include the list price plus 25¢ a copy to cover mailing costs.

Name_____

Address_____

City_____State_____Zip Code_____
Please allow at least 3 weeks for delivery